Praise for Peter Murphy's
The Last Weekend of the Summer:

"Thought provoking, sometimes humorous, sometimes agitating, this is a true slice of life being part of a family of flawed humans."
– Tome Tender

"An ode to summer, well-written read."
– Comfy Chair Books

"Will tug on your heart strings!"
– CMash Reads

"A very touching and emotional story!"
– Wall-to-Wall Books

"*The Last Weekend of the Summer* is a powerful and compelling story written from the heart. It is a must read that will make you ponder your own family dynamic, stir your soul, and resonate with you for a very long time."
– Jersey Girl Book Reviews

Flowers in the Snow

Flowers in the Snow

Peter Murphy

THE
ST●RY
PLANT

Also by Peter Murphy:

Lagan Love
Born & Bred
Wandering in Exile
All Roads
The Last Weekend of the Summer

For Cheryl, Kathleen, and Lou,
three of the best friends a writer could have.

And, of course, Alla,
who made me stop and think about what it would
really be like.

The Story Plant
Studio Digital CT, LLC
P.O. Box 4331
Stamford, CT 06907

Story Plant paperback ISBN-13: 978-1-61188-294-0
Fiction Studio Books E-book ISBN: 978-1-945839-33-7

Visit our website at www.TheStoryPlant.com

First Story Plant Printing: November 2020

Printed in the United States of America

0 9 8 7 6 5 4 3 2 1

The Family Tree

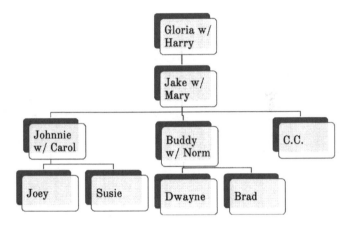

"Let the wind
take all that should be forgotten
and leave us only
with what should be remembered"

Chapter 1

Gloria stood by her kitchen window and waited for the kettle to boil. It was only five thirty, but she was afraid to go back to sleep. She'd had that terrible nightmare again.

It was still dark outside and would be for a few more hours. It had been a cold night, too. It was only the beginning of November, but already northern Muskoka was settling into winter; a time for hibernation, a time for deep and silent contemplation.

It was such a stark contrast to the hot, humid summers when her grandchildren would come with their children and fill her days with their laughter and, on more than a few occasions after their father had left, their tears. But if her long life had taught her anything, Gloria knew to enjoy each season as it came.

Over the years she had learned to adapt to when life was stripped down to the bare essentials of doing only what was really necessary and, if it had to be done outside, getting it done as quickly as possible. Once she had gotten used to all of that, she often had time on her hands.

Before, after her only son had gone off to boarding school and it was just her and Harry, she spent her free time painting for hours on end without any interruption. Then, when the need to interact with the outside world intruded, all she had to do was to put on her snow shoes, her warmest coat, hat and gloves, and take a brisk walk through the brilliant, white, emptiness of the world. She loved walking among the leafless trees leaving nothing but the tracks of her snowshoes along the trails where wolves had followed the spoor of rummaging deer.

Even as she aged, Gloria still found her walks invigorating and they allowed her to spend some time alone with the memories of her late husband. They had both loved the silence of those days but since her son Jake had died, Gloria had found that silence had become accusatory.

She shivered again and walked over to the thermostat. Her grandson had set it to an energy saving mode. It was lower overnight and would warm up again at seven. Johnnie had shown her how to alter the settings, but she could never remember. Instead, she just cranked up the dial.

Beneath the floor boards, the furnace rumbled back to life. It banged and clanged a few times, and then settled into a muffled roar. Soon currents of warmer air were gusting up through the vents and quickly made her kitchen cozy again. Johnnie had upgraded the insulation in the walls a few years back and the windows were triple glazed. They did keep the cold draughts out but this morning, they just made her reflection seem vague and unsure. She looked like a ghost trapped between worlds.

She walked over and turned off the lights and slowly felt her way back to the window. Outside, the sickle moon was waning but in the low light that remained, the snowscape seemed a blueish white, thick and lush, and undisturbed except where it had been cleared. The veranda had been shoveled but every morning it was coated with a new dusting of snow, mostly blown in from the lake. So was the walk to the dock where everything had been stored away in the boathouse, or under strongly bound tarps. It had to be kept clear too or, over the winter, the accumulating weight would do damage. It was heavy and constant work, but the man who ploughed the road did it for a small addition to his fees.

In the open spaces, the snow lay where it had fallen. Contoured by the winds, it gently rose and fell all the way down to the frozen shore were shards of thin, brittle ice had been driven to the shore to shrivel and die. Further out, the surface of the lake was solid ice under a thick blanket of soft, settled snow that lay undisturbed, except for the prints of her snowshoes. Almost every day since the lake had frozen over, she walked out to the spot where Jake's body had been found. She couldn't help herself; it was something she just had to do.

In her dream, he rose from the depths like he had changed his mind. He came all the way to the surface, but he could never break through. Then, on realizing he was trapped, he would look up at her and make sounds she couldn't hear. Frantically, she scratched at the ice but she could never break through to him in time.

She shivered again and pulled her robe tighter. She wished it was later so that she could wake Mary and have some company, but it was far too early. Besides, she needed to be in the right frame of mind to handle her daughter-in-law and all of her emotional rollercoasting.

Regardless of that, Gloria was happy that she had agreed to stay with her after Jake died. It had been an adjustment at first, but Gloria had offered and Mary had been more than happy to accept.

Poor Mary, the last weekend of the summer had been so hard on her. When the truth about her old infidelity surfaced, all of her years playing the victim had been exposed as the fraud Gloria always knew they were. That wasn't what Gloria had wanted. When she had arranged for Jake to visit, one last time, all she had hoped for was that he might find closure with the family he had been estranged from for years. She had also hoped that Mary could finally come to terms with all that had really happened.

Since her marriage had dissolved, Mary had become lost in the veils of her own deceits and the worst part was she demanded that her children take her side without question. It was very wrong of her and yet it was understandable: she had to appease her guilt. But all of that began to dissipate the night she sat and talked with the dying Jake. Gloria was happy about that part; happy that Mary and her son had been able to make their peace right before the end. For Mary it was a fragile peace, but at least it was something.

She held up well when the police arrived and answered all the questions they had to ask. Why had Jake gone out in the canoe alone? Had Gloria and Mary tried to do enough to dissuade him? Was Jake dealing with any undue stress or other issues? Despite her grief, Gloria had also remained firm through it all and shielded Mary as much as she could. "She is in shock," she had explained to the police. "We both are. Please respect that." They did, especially after Gloria used some old family connections to those in higher places.

The investigation into Jake's death was quickly concluded and returned an official verdict of 'misadventure.' After that, all that remained was to carry out Jake's final instructions. He had asked to be cremated and have his ashes thrown to the wind from the same cliff the children had spent so many summer afternoons jumping from. He had not specified who should do it and after his children talked about it, C.C. stepped forward with all of her steely determination and demanded she be allowed to take part. Johnnie also insisted, so Buddy was happy to step back. She remained in the cottage with Mary and Gloria, offering tea and commiserations while her husband, Norm, kept the kids occupied. Their children, Dwayne and Brad, were too young and were kept in the dark, while Johnnie's kids, Joey and Susie, were old enough to know to stay at the edge of everything.

Johnnie's wife, Carol, managed the kitchen and all the arrangements that had been overlooked, but she was distant, or reticent. Gloria had wanted to talk with her about that but right after C.C. and Johnnie returned, everyone seemed to be in such a hurry to get back to the city. They said it was because the school year had just begun and the children needed to get back into their routine, but Gloria knew it was far more than that.

Surprisingly, Mary had little to say about everyone leaving. Surprising, and not so surprising, to Gloria. Mary had fallen from her pedestal and would need time and space to find her composure, and a new role in her family's life.

The kettle began to whistle and Gloria made her way towards the stove and turned on the hood light. She made her favorite tea and sat by her large, polished table and prepared for another day.

The tea brought her some comfort. Almost enough to dispel the lingering horror of her dream, but there was still her guilt and remorse. She should not have accepted Jake's decision so easily. She had tried to talk him out of it. They had talked for hours on the phone, from when he was first diagnosed through to when he decided to forego any more treatment. His reasoning was solid and she could not find a compelling argument against it. But she should have. She should have fought for the life she had given him. Maybe if she had been able to find the right words, he might have reconsidered. Who knows? He could have prolonged the battle. He could have lived for a few more years. But he was in constant pain. And he looked like a man who was dying.

As a younger man, Jake had always been so conscious of his appearance. He was not the type who could tolerate being seen as a sick, withering man. They had talked about that and he had told her that he had not wanted his children to remember him like that. At least Gloria had been able to talk him past that. At least there was that.

She sipped from her tea cup and tried to dwell on that little piece of solace, but Jake's face rose from the depths inside of her, pleading with his mother to do for him what he could not do for himself. She had not done what a mother should have done and there was nobody left that she could talk with about that. And certainly not Mary, she had more than enough on her plate.

"Have you been up long?" Mary asked as she came into the kitchen, turning on all of the lights as she passed. She didn't wait for an answer and turned the kettle back on before walking towards the window. She looked out towards the lake, but quickly turned away. She looked around the room like she was searching for things to rearrange and on finding none, settled on Gloria. "You should not be getting up so early. At your age, you should be getting more rest. What am I to tell the kids if you let yourself get run down? They will get after me, you know. They will say that I should have taken better care of you."

Without waiting for Gloria to respond, Mary checked the thermostat. "It was a very cold night, are you sure you are warm enough? I could get you a blanket." And before Gloria said anything, Mary walked over and touched the back of her hand. "You must be cold. You really should not be sitting down here when you could have stayed in your nice, warm bed. You could have called out to me and I would have brought your tea up to you. I am quite able, you know."

Gloria shook her head and said nothing. Mornings with Mary were often a little hectic. In the first few days after Jake died, she had gone into a shell and wandered around like a ghost. Gloria had let her be for a while. She knew that Mary needed time to grieve, for herself and for her long dormant love for a man who was now dead.

In time, Mary began to recover her composure and her resolve. From now on, she had explained in a long, heartfelt outpouring of everything Jake's passing had stirred up, she would begin every day full of vigor and resolve. She would honor what they had once been by no longer allowing herself to be what she had become. And where she had long been a whiner and a complainer, she was now determined to become a cheerful bringer of comfort, every single moment of the day.

Some days, she almost managed. Other days, not so much. On the bad days something would trip her up and she would indulge in a little pity party until Gloria coaxed her out of it, reminding her daughter-in-law of all the progress she had made.

She had come a long way. Since the day Johnnie and C.C. had spread Jake's ashes, she had not once spoken badly about him. Instead, she had become the villain in her own life and when her efforts to change wore thin, she would berate herself mercilessly until Gloria intervened and redirected her.

It was easy. Mary was at her happiest when she was busy and cleaned the cottage almost every single day, vacuuming and dusting, fluffing pillows and rearranging bric-a-brac. She even climbed up on a chair to clean the inside of the windows every few days.

At first, Gloria found it a little annoying, but she understood. Mary had to make her amends. To help her in that, Gloria made a point of leaving her tea-cup in the living room, or she would leave her reading glasses upstairs for Mary to fetch, and she even stopped doing the laundry and ironing.

Sometimes, Gloria felt a little guilty about that—and a little put out. Ironing had always been one of those activities that was very soothing in its monotony. And it reaffirmed her independence. She could still look after herself, even at her age. She relinquished all of that, she reminded herself, because Mary needed activity, and distraction.

Besides, it was doing Mary the world of good. She lost almost fifteen pounds and had not sniffed and flicked her head in weeks. She was the healthiest and happiest she had been in years.

Except for one thing; she was avoiding her children and they seemed to be avoiding her.

"Are you ready for breakfast?" Mary asked after she had taken just a few sips from her tea. "I could make us both some nice scrambled eggs?"

Gloria was not one for eating much before noon, but she nodded and smiled. "That would be lovely, especially with some toast and the new jam." They had made a new batch together and while it wasn't as good as the jams Gloria made on her own, she knew Mary was proud of it.

"Yes, that would be perfect. One egg, or two?"

"Just one, thank you."

"One? That is hardly enough."

Gloria might have asked why Mary had even offered her the choice, but decided to let it go. "Very well. Two, please, but it can wait until you have finished your tea."

"Not at all," Mary replied like the idea was heretical. She rose with energy and purpose and was soon the center of a whirl of activity, talking constantly and never waiting for Gloria to respond. It didn't matter, Gloria had other things on her mind.

In the kitchen of a beautifully restored house in one of the recently gentrified neighborhoods of Toronto, Johnnie had made his first pot of coffee. He would drink a couple of cups before he brought one up to Carol. Then he would wake Joey and Susie.

He didn't need to be up so early; it was habit. Work always slowed down at this time of the year. No one wanted renovations going on over Christmas and the few jobs that remained were almost finished. He had the plumber scheduled for the kitchen remodel in Cabbagetown, the electrician just needed some light fixtures for the store in Summerhill, and the painters were ready to start on Mount Pleasant. He would drop by each one, but he would do it later in the morning. Beyond that, his day was clear.

Normally at this time of the year, he would take a few days off and head up to Gloria's. He could always find something to do around the old, rambling cottage, but this year was different. His mother was there and, after talking with Carol, he had decided that Mary was probably best left alone for a while yet—to try to regain her composure, if nothing else.

Johnnie had a few misgivings about that but since his father's death, he had gone into a bit of a funk and was beginning to rethink his whole relationship with his family. He used to take pride in that he had always been the reliable one—the one who could always deal with what the rest of them could not. It was the role that he had been forced to assume when he was a child and his father had left. But when his father came back and asked Johnnie to help him kill himself . . .

Jake had tried to make it sound like it was no different than putting down an old dog that was suffering, but Johnnie couldn't. Nor could he forget the look of disappointment on his father's face.

When he talked with Carol about it, she had done what she had always done before. She heard him out and then tried to help him past it. She had reassured him that he had done the right thing and in a clumsy effort to lift his mood, she had reminded him that he hadn't even been able to do that when their old Lab was at its end; that she was the one who had to take him to the vet. She wasn't belittling him or what he was going through; she was just making her point.

He had tried to laugh at that, but he couldn't. Deep down, he was too damned angry. He was angry at his father for asking him to do that, he was angry at his mother for all the years she forced him to fill in for his father, and he was angry at his sisters.

"It might be better for all concerned if you stayed out of their lives for a while," Carol had suggested when he told her about those feelings. "I think they all need to come to terms with everything that has happened, and they might be better off doing it on their own."

She was right. Buddy, and C.C., had always been more than happy to drag him into every little drama they found themselves in. And she was right when she suggested that he might also be angry with himself for always enabling them, but he just couldn't help himself. They were family, after all.

He drained his cup and rose to refill it when he heard Carol moving around upstairs. Today was the day she was making their pitch on the old cinema project. The whole thing was to be restored to its nineteen-thirties' grandeur. It was the type of project that Johnnie had always dreamed of working on.

He had just poured a second cup and left it on the counter when his phone vibrated. He picked it up and smiled as he read the text. *Thanks for last night, Bro. It was just what I needed. XOXOXO.*

"From one of your girlfriends?" Carol asked as she came in and headed straight for the coffee.

Johnnie was caught out for a moment, but answered quickly: "What can I say? I am a walking babe-magnet."

He gave her his best wry smile, but avoided looking into her eyes. "Are Joey and Susie not down, yet?"

"Do you see them?" Carol joked, and struggled to control her face as she watched him stuff his phone into his pocket.

"Okay, then. I'll just go up and wake them," Johnnie muttered as he hurried past her.

After he had woken the kids, and poured more coffee into a travel mug, he grabbed his keys and his phone. "Have a great day," he offered with his best boyish smile and kissed her on the cheek. "And get us that damn cinema job."

Chapter 2

When Buddy woke, she tried to be as quiet as she could. She did not want to disturb Norm. He'd had another fitful night, tossing and turning, and muttering in his sleep. It had been happening for the last week, or so. Buddy had tried to talk with him about it, but he said it was nothing for her to be concerned about; that it was just some crazy dreams. She had decided to let it go at that for now because she didn't want to rock the boat.

She quietly found her robe and slippers and went downstairs to get breakfast ready. The kids would be happy with juice and cereal, but she wanted to make something special for Norm. She decided on waffles; he always ordered them whenever they went to The Pickle Barrel. She also had some turkey bacon, which she could microwave, and she could smother the whole thing with maple syrup, just the way he liked it.

Everything was ready by the time he came down. He looked at her and smiled but she could tell, it was just reflex. He went straight to the coffee pot and filled the mug she had left there for him. It was the Toronto Maple Leaf one she had picked out for the kids to give him on Father's Day. "I made breakfast," she said and held up the plate with the waffles and bacon.

He checked his watch and had a pained expression on his face. "I don't have time. I have to get to the office early."

"But I made it for you."

"And I really appreciate that, but I can't. Things are getting really hectic at work and I have to get there early. And I'll probably be late this evening, too."

"How late?"

"I have no idea, but I will give you a call." He drained his mug without looking at her. He seemed conflicted for a moment, then headed for the front door. "Hey kids," he shouted up the stairs. "Be good boys for your mother and I will see you later." Without waiting for their response, he left.

Buddy sighed and sat down at her kitchen table, picking absentmindedly at the turkey bacon. At the very least, he could have kissed her cheek before he left. Or he could have given her a hug. Or he could have tried one piece of bacon before he rushed off. She nibbled at the corner of a waffle and tried not to cry. Since they had their big meltdown at the end of the summer, things had been going so much better—after they had a chance to talk it all through. She had been as honest as she could be and they had agreed not to give up on each other. She had told him that she was now able to see how she had been taking all of her frustrations out on him and that she now realized how unfair that had been.

It felt good to say it. It felt like she was steeping out of the shadows she had been hiding in for years, but it also made her feel vulnerable and afraid.

He had been so good about it. He had taken her in his arms and held her close. He said he'd always understood and that he should have been more patient with her. He also said they were both at fault for the way things had been and from now on, he was going to do whatever he had to do to try to make things better between them.

After her father died, and she had gone through a whole whirlwind of emotions, Norm had gone out of his way to be there for her. He had listened as she poured out all of her anger and guilt—and her shame for having such bitter feelings towards someone who had just died. He had told her it was okay to have those feelings. "Everybody goes through them. They call it the stages of grief," he had explained and promised her that he would try to be there for her through all of them.

He had tried harder than she had any right to expect. In fact, it was like he had become a whole new man. For the first few weeks, he did everything with the kids. He dropped them off at school in the mornings, even though it meant he got to the office late. And he took them to hockey practice in the evening and stood around in the cold while they flopped and floundered on the ice. But none of that made her feel better about herself. If anything, it made her feel worse. It made her feel like she was acting like a spoiled child who had to be humored.

She had tried telling herself not to think that way; that it was just her old negativity. She even talked with Norm about that.

"Neural networks," he had answered, and she knew he was trying to sound serious and thoughtful. "I just read a very interesting article somewhere that said that negative thinking creates some type of pathway in our brains and after a while we just follow it automatically without being aware. The article also said that we have to deliberately force ourselves to change that."

"Did the article say anything about how to deal with the damage done by toxic mothers?" Buddy had asked, less unkindly than it had sounded. She was beginning to come to terms with that part of her problem—at least at a cognitive level. Like any child, she had only ever wanted her mother's approval and the only way she had ever been able to get it was by playing along with all of Mary's umbrage and outrage—her imagined and self-serving umbrage and outrage as it now turned out.

"Don't be so hard on her," Norm had coaxed her. "She was just reacting to the cards life dealt her."

Buddy hadn't meant to react the way she did. She had just stood and stared at him like he was taking sides against her. It was all very well for him to act all philosophical and rational about it all but for her, it was still personal; deeply personal.

Later, when she was alone, she had stormed around her kitchen ranting and raging against all of the negativity her mother had poured into her life. As a child, Buddy had grown so used to all of her mother's bouts of self-pity and rationalization, all of her ranting and raving against her father, and all of the now blatant lies and accusations Mary had used to deflect her own guilt. Buddy had become so used to it all that she had grown up to become someone just like that.

With such an example, what else could she do?

And she had also allowed herself to become the victim in her own life.

When Mary decided that she would live with Gloria, Buddy was relieved. She wasn't sure how she might have behaved if her mother had moved in with them.

Norm was happy about it too, and not for all the selfish reasons he'd had before. He now said it would give them the time and space to sort things out in their own lives. "It's not that I want to sound like I am critical of my mother-in-law," he had joked to lighten the mood. "But . . ."

"But what; that she is always taking my side?" Buddy decided to play along.

"Exactly."

"And what is the problem with that?"

"Because," he reached over and pulled her to his chest. "That's my job."

He was right. She did need to take some time away from her mother. Johnnie had said the same thing, over and over—almost every time she talked with him. He also told her that Carol wanted him to stay out of everybody's lives for a while. Buddy said she understood, but sometimes she caught herself resenting Carol for that.

She caught herself resenting her mother, too. Mary had always been so reliant on her and now, after everything had been dragged out into the open, Mary had taken off and left Buddy to try to sort out the whole mess on her own.

"I don't mean to sound like I am blaming her for everything," she had explained to Norm over dinner one evening. They had gone out and left the kids with Susie. It was part of Norm's plan for how they would get out of the rut: they would start having date nights again. They had taken a cab, too, so Norm could relax and have a few drinks.

"You're so sexy when you're pouting." He laughed and made his love-sick face. He was on his second glass of wine and was getting a little frisky.

"Be serious, for a moment."

"Sorry. That is something I cannot do, right now."

"And why is that?"

"Because I am out on a date with my beautiful, sexy wife." He tried to top up her glass, but she moved it away.

"Down boy. I have already decided that we are doing it tonight. But I really do need to talk about this stuff."

"I know, but right now I think you need to take a break from it."

"If only it was that easy."

"It is. Have some more wine."

This time, she let him pour some more and raised the glass to her lips. He was right. She had to learn to stop gnawing at it. She sipped some wine and tried to think of something else to say. They had also agreed not to talk about the kids, at least for the rest of the evening.

"So, how are things at work? When are they going to give you that big promotion they have been promising you? Now that C.C. got hers, I might need something to brag about."

"What can I tell you, the world has turned against men like me. It's all about empowering women these days. Besides, it's the weekend and I don't want to think about work until the alarm goes off on Monday morning. Let's talk about something else."

"Okay, then. What would you like to talk about?"

"Okay, then. What about the Leafs? Three wins in a row. They're going all the way this year."

"All the way where?" Buddy asked as she had done every other time. It had become a stock routine between them.

"The Stanley Cup, babe. This is going to be their year."

"You know you have been saying that since we first started going out together?"

"And one of these years I will be right. Hey, maybe we should try and get tickets some evening. You and me together at the hockey game. How much more romantic could it get?"

Buddy decided to play along, it felt so warm and . . . it felt like the way things were when they had first started going out. "Norm, as much as I would love to go and watch hockey with you . . ."

"But?"

"Wouldn't you rather go see the game with Johnnie?"

"Can't. He's not allowed to play with me right now."

"Carol?"

"Yup, not that I blame her."

"How does Johnnie feel about that?"

"Hard to say, he's more of a baseball guy."

"So, we are not going to talk about that, either?"

"Nope?"

"So, what is left that we can talk about?"

He seemed to be at a loss for a moment, but then sipped his wine and smiled. "What would you do if we won a million dollars?"

"Really, Norm?"

"Yeah, really."

"I'd pay off the mortgage."

"Wrong."

"I'd set up college funds for the kids."

"Wrong."

"Okay then, what would you do?"

"I'd build a tree fort in our yard."

"Isn't there a song about that?"

"Yup, and I would hire the band to follow me around and sing that song all day long."

"Norm."

"What?"

"I love you. I don't deserve you, but I love you."

"Aww, shucks."

But since then, something had changed. For the last few weeks, Norm always seemed to be so stressed out, and he was having all those bad dreams. He was spending all of his time at the office. She had tried to talk with him about it, but he wouldn't and that just made things worse. Buddy began to reexamine everything that had happened between them. She must have done something—or said something.

*

By the time he got to the office, Norm was already feeling fried. He felt bad about rushing out on Buddy, but he couldn't tell her yet—not until it was confirmed.

"Got a minute?" Jack called out to him. Norm had just sat down and attached his laptop. He hadn't even had time to grab a coffee. He rose and walked over to Jack's corner office. It was large and furnished like something out of a magazine. It was bare and sterile, devoid of any personal effects like family photos, or pictures of Jack holding a prize fish, or framed, signed posters of athletes—all the things Norm would have put up if it was his.

"Close the door," Jack said casually, without looking up. He was the top guy in the Canadian office and reported only to the CEO in Dallas. Norm closed the door and waited to be invited to sit. Jack was okay, but there was something ominous about it all. Rumors had been flying around the office for days and everybody feared the worst.

"I just wanted to give you a head's up," Jack finally looked up and smiled while gesturing to Norm to take a seat in a stiff, tubular chair. Nothing in the office was made of wood; everything was metal, cold, hard, shiny metal.

"What's up?" Norm asked. He tried to make it sound casual, but there was a slight quaver in his voice.

If Jack noticed, he didn't let on. "It hasn't been made official yet, but we will be closing down all of the Canadian operations. Starting in January, we are going to run everything from Texas."

"Everything?"

"That's the plan."

"And what will that mean for everybody here? Will we be asked to relocate?"

"Probably not. We have successfully completed the outsourcing of all logistic and customer support functions. After Christmas, they will be managed from the Dallas office."

It was like a kick in the guts. Norm had headed up those transition projects believing that when they were complete, he would be rewarded with something; a promotion, or a transfer. Anything but this.

"I am telling you because I wanted you to have a head start. It might not be the best time of the year for a job hunt, but what can you do? You will receive a generous severance package—and your bonus. And," Jack leaned forward as if to add a more human touch. "I have recommended that you get fifteen percent this year."

"I see," Norm answered as the news swirled around inside of him. "Thank you," he added, more from reflex than real conviction.

"Don't thank me. You earned every penny," Jack smiled his plastic smile while Norm felt like the room was spinning around him. Spinning faster and faster and leaving him a little nauseated.

"You know it is not personal," Jack added when Norm didn't react. "It's just business." He picked up some papers from his desk and Norm took his cue. He rose and headed for the door.

"It would be better if the others didn't know until it is officially announced," Jack added without looking up from his papers. "By increasing your bonus, we are hoping that you will be on board with whatever might be required to make the transition as smooth as possible. Who knows, if things go well, I might even be able to squeeze out another one or two percent."

Norm nodded and left. He poured himself a coffee and walked back to his cubicle. The others began to file in and he greeted them as he always did. He would give nothing away, at least not until he had finished digesting it all. But how was he going to tell Buddy?

Maybe, he wouldn't have to, he decided after some thought. He had built up a solid reputation and some-one like him could always find something. Right after his coffee, he would make a few calls.

In a way, he reasoned as he forced himself to re-main calm, Jack had done him a favor—letting him know in advance. But, deep down, it didn't really feel like that. Deep down, it felt like he had just been stabbed in the back.

Chapter 3

Even before she opened her eyes, C.C. was thinking about Heather. She was thinking about the way she lay on her pillow, with her hair tussled, and her face half buried but always managing to look so stunningly beautiful. Just thinking about her always brought a smile to C.C.'s face.

She would have given anything to be able to reach out and touch that angelic face. She would have given anything to be able to gently stroke those soft cheeks until Heather's eyelids began to stir while C.C. waited like an excited child; waiting for Heather to open her bright, blue eyes.

C.C. would have given anything, but instead she turned the other way so she could see her bedside clock. Once again, she had woken alone in her wide, empty bed. But at least she had woken before the alarm went off. It was a small consolation, but she could find something comforting in that.

Before, she would have jumped up and begun her morning flurry. She would have rushed into the kitchen and started the coffee machine. She would have hurried back to her bedroom and turned on the TV. She would have paused for a moment while she checked the business headlines. Then she would have gone to her bathroom and turned on the shower until everything became steamy while she brushed her teeth in the part of the mirror she kept clear with her fingers.

After she had showered, she would have wrapped herself in her long white robe. Then she would have made her way back to the kitchen and poured her first coffee of the day; Jamaican Blue Mountain, because she was worth it. Then, she would have savored every mouthful as she reviewed her agenda for the day. But she didn't do any of that. Instead, she just lay there.

Heather hadn't stayed over in a few weeks. She said she was busy with her studies and C.C. had said she understood. She did, but a part of her was hurt— the part of her that she had taken to calling her girly-side. She had talked with Johnnie about that and he had just laughed at her.

"I didn't realize that lesbians had a feminine side."

Her old self would have risen to that, even if it was only their usual brother/sister banter. But she was changing. Her old self had been the hard shell she had worn against the world and now the way she looked at the world had been changed—totally and utterly changed.

And it wasn't just Heather's influence. For most of her thirty odd years C.C. had lived believing that her own father had so little interest in her. She had grown up believing that he had preferred her brother and sister. She had lived for all those years remembering only the pained expression on his face whenever he looked at her.

She really only remembered him from the few times he had come to spend part of the summer with them at the cottage—just for a few weeks every August when she was a child— but it was enough to teach her that the world wasn't going to be fair with her. It was enough to teach her that nothing could be taken for granted and that if she wanted something from life, she would have to take it without compassion or consideration for anyone else. They were weaknesses she had disdained because life had also taught her how to harden herself against her own heart.

That was something Heather forced her to come to terms with right after Jake had died and C.C. needed to talk about it because she was feeling totally and utterly lost. The man she had believed was her father, wasn't. And then after he apologized for not loving her as his own anyway, he had gone and drowned himself. How the hell was she supposed to process that?

Her old self had wanted to lash out and make somebody pay. Right after she had found out that Jake wasn't her father, she had told Susie that it would be Buddy—for blurting it out. She had mentioned that to Heather, too, but she had just smiled. "Don't you think that Buddy's world has been turned upside down enough?" She had asked like she was talking to a child.

It felt like Heather was testing her so C.C. had decided to let it go and told herself that she just didn't have the energy for all of that, anymore. Instead, when she got back to the city, she immersed herself in her work while she processed it all. Everything she had grown up with had been turned upside down. Her mother, who had always been so sanctimonious and critical, had been exposed as the hypocrite C.C. always knew she was. And Buddy, her mother's little, goodie-two-shoed side-kick, had known all along.

The old C.C. would have made them both pay but because of Heather, she decided to try to look for a different way past all of that. Besides, everybody was keeping to themselves these days. That last weekend of the summer had done a number on them all.

It was one of the reasons Heather had given for not moving in with her just yet and it had a certain, indisputable logic. But C.C. was done with cold, hard thinking. She just wanted warm, mushy, comforting, romance. She wanted to trust in love and dive in at the deep end—despite everything life had taught her. She wanted to have someone else at the core of her existence and she wanted that someone to be Heather. She wanted to spend every moment of every day with her, but Heather still wouldn't move in with her. She said she wasn't ready. She said they weren't ready, and C.C. had to accept that.

It wasn't easy and C.C. often wondered if Heather wasn't just playing some version of hard-to-get. If she was, it was working. She was all that C.C. thought about. She had even begun to measure every single thing she did by what Heather might think; the way she dressed, the way she behaved at work, the way she spent her time and money, even the way she watched movies. She had to laugh at herself: she was becoming such a girl.

It's called growing up, Johnnie had told her in a late-night texting session when Carol was away visiting her family. *It happens to the best of us.*

And the worst.

Are we feeling a little sorry for ourselves these days?

I can't speak for you, but, if I am, I happen to have a very good reason. Someone just knocked my favorite chip off my shoulder. I am not sure whether I should be outraged, or offended.

I think you should go with both; I'm sure you could pull it off.

C.C. had laughed out loud at that. Johnnie always knew how to bring her out of her moods, but secretly she resented that they had to sneak around behind Carol's back to talk. Johnnie gave no clue as to how he felt about that, other than always being there for her like he had always done before.

C.C. had tried getting together with Carol, directly, but she had said she was busy. It might have been a brush-off, but there was also some truth in it. It was the time of the year when she had to start lining up jobs for the next year.

Johnnie and Carol were a great team and C.C. envied them for that. And she missed being able to spend time with them, but she and Susie had started to hang out and that was something. They had gone for brunch and shopping a few times and it had been a real blast. The kid was like both of her parents rolled into one. And she was a great source of information on what the rest of the family was up to as she had just recently started babysitting Buddy's kids, and she was always in touch with Gloria.

Sometimes, C.C. felt bad for pumping her teenage niece for scuttlebutt so she tried to balance her karma by buying the kid anything she wanted. And she bought some stuff for Joey, too, so he didn't feel left out. It was so much fun. She and Susie could never agree on what Joey might like so C.C. took to soliciting opinions from some of the cute, young guys in the mall.

It was so obvious and Susie was embarrassed at first, but she quickly started to play along.

"We are trying to pick out a sweater for her brother," C.C. had explained to a very ripped young guy who agreed to model a few for them. Susie had really gotten into it, especially when he agreed to try on a tight cashmere. He was a bit older than her, but he seemed to like her, too.

C.C. was just about to ask if he would like to join them for a coffee, or something, when it all fell apart. As he was rippling his way into the sweater, and his head had just popped through the neck, he let it slip that his boyfriend had one just like it.

"That was so embarrassing," Susie laughed after he had gone.

"Maybe he's just going through a phase."

Susie pretended to be shocked. "You know, if a straight person said that . . . besides, don't people like you have gaydar?"

"What do you mean by 'people like me'?"

"You know, interfering old aunts."

*

When the alarm did go off, C.C. rose reluctantly. She had scheduled a breakfast meeting near the airport. She was bringing together all of the Regional Sales Managers so they could personally report on the year so far. *A breakfast of champions*, she smirked at herself in the mirror. It would be the usual; a gathering of the old boys slyly trying to put their best spin on their bad news and openly claiming all responsibility for any that was good.

Before, she would have relished the idea of going in and terrorizing a few of them. They had never taken her seriously when she was in the field and, even after she had scampered past them on the corporate ladder, she had never forgotten that. It was a part of her job that she once enjoyed, but she could hardly be bothered anymore. She thought about just 'phoning it in,' but she couldn't. Her work ethic wouldn't allow it. As long as she was cashing the company's paychecks, she owed them her best. Especially now that the paychecks were bigger and she had her own corner office with her name and title on the door: V.P. Sales & Marketing.

She had been so excited about her promotion—it was everything the last few years had been about—but when she told Heather, she hadn't seemed so impressed. She had gone through the motions, but C.C. could tell. Heather valued other things in life. Humanness, compassion, empathy, all the things that C.C.'s years in corporate life had breed out of her.

They had gone out for dinner to celebrate and Heather had tried to make a fuss, even asking for details that she clearly didn't understand or care about. It almost made C.C. feel like a little child who had brought home a good report card and now, when she looked at her nameplate, it looked more like a large, scarlet 'A.' She was tempted to change it to 'Chief Corporate Barbie.' She had even joked about that with Susie.

"But that would set feminism back a few decades," her niece had answered, trying so hard to look serious and adult. "It would be like you were standing on top of the glass ceiling making faces at the rest of us."

"I'm sorry. I didn't realize that you had such strong feelings on the matter."

"I don't really, but I am going to go to college in a few years and I want to be able to blend in."

"Will you have to become a Vegan?"

"Maybe I already am."

"I didn't know that."

"Yeah, but I got to keep it on the down-low. If my mom found out . . ."

"How is your mom?"

Susie hesitated, so C.C. dragged her to a shoe store window—her favorite shoe store. "What do you think of those?" She had pointed to a pair of boots that would be perfect for someone as tall as Susie.

"Ugh; they are made of some poor animal's skin."

That, along with all of the things Heather had said, set off a cascade in C.C.'s mind that ultimately led to her questioning everything she was doing with her life.

It's just a mid-life crisis, Johnnie had told her when she shared that with him.

I am not old enough for one of those.

The world is changing fast, he had written back. *Thirty is the new fifty.*

The world was changing fast, or at least her world was. And it was all beginning to seem so one dimensional. Careerists like her never cluttered their work lives with personal details. It was all about what you had done—or claimed to have done—for the corporate good. It was all about getting the results, about meeting the numbers, and about delivering value to shareholders in the current quarter. Anything beyond that was somebody else's problem.

Heather was disdainful of things like that—and she didn't care for C.C.'s BMW. She had said that if it was what C.C. wanted, that she could live with it, but she would have preferred something more environmentally friendly. After that, C.C.'s shiny, little Barbie car never looked the same again.

Her instinctive reaction was to get pissed off, but C.C. couldn't allow herself to get angry at Heather. That was the way the old her would have reacted. First, she would have allowed herself a little outrage binge—just to vent, even if only to herself. But that was how it always began. Each little binge would chip something away and before long she would become contemptuous of the very thing she had once loved.

Besides, she had chided herself, outrage binges were more her mother's thing—and Buddy's.

She regretted even thinking that, especially when she considered how Heather would have reacted if she knew. Heather valued forgiveness and giving second chances, things that C.C. had never given a single thought to. She had always kept score, but all of that would have to change if their love was going to last. It would mean going against every instinct she had developed.

"Sucks to be in love," Johnnie teased her when she had shared those thoughts with him.

"How do you manage?"

"The patterns for a man/woman relationship have been established long ago. You kids, and your new-fangled same-sex relationship stuff are in uncharted territory."

"Like one of us should brow beat the other?"

"Yup. Now you just have to figure out who does what to who?"

"You know you sound like Norm when you talk like that. And speaking of our dear brother-in-law, how is the loveable pervert?"

"Haven't seen him in a few months."

"Are you guys avoiding each other?"

"No. Like they say in relationship therapy: we are just giving each other time and space. He and Buddy have some sorting out to do."

"You are such a liberated man, but I have to ask: is there a lesson in that for me?"

"Always."

"You know that Heather hasn't told her parents about us yet?"

"Can't say that I blame her."

"She says she will when the time is right, but I am having a hard time with that. Now, the old me would demand to know when, but the new me . . . I'm just trying to go with the flow."

"Good luck with that."

"I know. I am still pissed that I had to spend Thanksgiving alone. What did you guys do?"

"We spent it with Carol's family."

"Must be nice."

"C.C., we all agreed to let this one pass. It was too soon after Dad died."

"Yeah, I guess it was."

"You going to be okay, Sis?"

"You know me, Bro."

"I do. That's why I am asking."

"Love you too, Bro, and now I got to run."

Chapter 4

Gloria and Mary were spending another afternoon in the heated, enclosed part of the veranda, reading and sipping tea. They had made the trek down to the local stores and stocked up for the next week, or so. Gloria was too old to drive, and Mary was still far too nervous on the icy roads, so the man who ploughed the snow had taken them.

It had become a regular thing, and he checked in on them almost every single day. His father had been one of the few neighbors Harry had allowed to get close to him. They had both fought in the war and, as they grew old together, enjoyed spending their summer evenings sitting together on the dock in almost total silence. Yet when they did speak, it seemed to Gloria that they were carrying on an ongoing conversation, one they stretched out for over a decade.

Her afternoons with Mary were becoming like that, except the words they shared were of no real importance. It was like they were just making little noises to remind each other that they were not alone. Mary more so. Even when she was reading, she could not remain quiet. At first, Gloria thought it was an effort to start a conversation. It never was. It was a more like a running commentary on what the author had written. It could be funny, but it could also become a little annoying.

Mary would not have been Gloria's ideal choice of companion for such cabin-bound days, but she couldn't even think about saying or doing anything to make her feel unwelcome. Mary was in hiding from the rest of the world. She was clearly avoiding contact with her children, except for the obligatory calls to ask after her grandchildren.

Gloria was growing more and more concerned about that and had taken to eavesdropping. She did it without a second thought and when her conscience got to her, she reminded herself that she was only doing it for Mary's own good. She was, after all, merely monitoring Mary's progress.

In all fairness, other than that, Mary was doing so well. She was staying active, even on the worst days, and had lost a few more pounds. And she remembered how to smile again. From the first day Jake had brought her home, Gloria always told Mary that she had such a pretty smile.

For the most part, Mary seemed as happy as could be expected, except when she came back from her walks on the lake. She had also taken to visiting the spot where Jake's body had been found—where he had washed up like a piece of driftwood on the rocky shore of the island. She would smile bravely, but Gloria could see that it was strained.

Sometimes, Mary would look at Gloria to see if it was time to talk about what had happened, but Gloria always had to look away. She wasn't ready to deal with all of that and somedays it felt like she never would. Somedays she just felt too old and that her loss had been too great, but she knew she would have to try to find a way, for everybody's sake.

It worried her that the family had all gone their separate ways and were in no hurry to see each other again but, as Gloria had to admit to herself, she and Mary were not setting a very good example. They were behaving like two fugitives hiding out in a cabin in the woods until things cooled off.

"Have you given any thought to what we should do about Christmas?" she asked as she put her book away. It was another matter that had lingered in the air between them.

Mary took a moment before she looked up from her book. "I have. Have you?"

"Some."

"And?"

It was going to be one of those conversations where Gloria would have to pull every word from her daughter-in-law's mouth. It was understandable. In the whirlwind of emotions that followed Jake's passing, the issue of him not being C.C.'s biological father had been shuffled into the background. Gloria had suspected it all along, but she had never believed that any good would come from confronting Mary about it. And she certainly wasn't going to do that now. It was a discussion for another day, and it was one for Mary and her children to try to have.

Johnnie would probably be fine with it—once he had sorted out his own reactions to not being able to honor his father's strange request. Buddy would probably muddle through, as well, even if it meant she would have to take her mother down from the pedestal. Besides, she had her own issues to deal with.

C.C.? Now that would be another story. Since her initial shock and outrage, she had gone back into her own life and would surface again when she was ready. And, if the past was anything to go by, there might be hell to pay. Gloria might have to find a way of heading her off but right now, her major concern was Mary.

Before, in the throes of self-righteousness, Mary had never hesitated to play the pity card and insist that her children constantly reassure her of their loyalties. She couldn't do that anymore and was now probably dreading their reactions—or even their total rejection. Gloria would have to do something about that, too.

"Maybe it is time that we all got together again. Don't you think enough time has passed?" Gloria asked as a plan began to form in her mind.

"And how do you think the children might feel about it?" Mary had put down her book, but didn't make eye-contact.

"I think that the children will be fine with it."

"How can you be so sure?"

"Because of your grandchildren. No matter what we may be going through, we must celebrate Christmas for their sake. And no Christmas could be complete if the children didn't spend time with their grandmother."

"And their great grandmother."

"That goes without saying," Gloria laughed a little. She had been dreading having to raise the matter, but Mary seemed to be okay with it; okay enough to at least talk about it. What she would be able to cope with would be another matter.

"So, it is settled then?"

Mary picked her book up again and sighed. "I think we should wait and see what the others have to say."

"Sometimes a matriarch must lead, even when she doesn't know the way."

Gloria meant it as a joke, but Mary's face clouded over.

"Even if it means forcing people to do what they are not ready to do?" She answered with more than a hint of recrimination, but that was to be expected. Mary was still a bit reticent that Gloria had arranged Jake's final visit without telling her.

"If we didn't, the entire world would still be running around in diapers."

Mary did smile at that, but it was obvious that she wasn't convinced.

Gloria decided to let it go for now. She had planted the seed. She would let it settle and come back to water it regularly. In the meantime, she had other seeds to sow. But she would come back to Mary, only she would take a very different approach. One that might force Mary to step up and reclaim her dignity with her own family.

She excused herself and went inside to make a telephone call.

"Dad?" Susie asked. She tried to make it sound offhand and casual so she didn't look over at him.

Her father was driving her to the mall. C.C. had offered to swing by and pick her up, but Susie wanted a chance to talk with her father alone. Things between them hadn't been the same since his father died. Susie often tried to imagine what he must be going through, but she couldn't.

She had talked with Gloria about it and her great grandmother had been quick to tell her there was no cause to be worried, but it almost sounded like she was unsure of herself, too. It seemed like the whole family was getting lost and nobody knew what to do about that. If only they could get back to the way things used to be.

"Yeah?"

"Have you thought about Christmas?"

"I have, and I have a long list of all the things I want from Santa."

"I just want one thing."

It felt a bit childish, but Susie was sure it would work. Besides, her father had started it, talking about Santa.

"Really?"

"Yes, Daddy."

He hesitated for a moment and she worried that she might have overplayed it. 'Daddy'! What was she thinking? She hadn't called him that in years.

"I see."

"Don't you want to know what it is?"

"I think I have a fairly good idea."

"So, can we?"

"I don't know."

"Aww, please?"

"Have you talked with your mother?"

"Not yet."

"Well, we'll have to wait and see what she says."

"If she says 'Yes,' can we?"

He didn't answer as they turned into the mall parking lot. It was already full and there were a few cars prowling for empty spots. C.C. had said she would be waiting by the main door.

"So, can we?"

"Did she put you up to this," he asked when they saw C.C. waving.

"No. She doesn't even know about it."

Johnnie brought the truck to a standstill and leaned over so his daughter could kiss him on the cheek.

"Can we?" Susie repeated.

"If your mother says okay."

"You're the best dad in the world." Susie almost squealed as she hugged him so tightly.

*

"Did he give you money, or something?" C.C. asked after Johnnie had driven away and Susie had stood waving until he was gone. "You didn't have to ask him, you know. You have a rich aunt who loves spoiling you."

"I know," Susie turned and smiled. "That's why I didn't ask him for money."

"What did you ask for?" C.C. smiled back. There were times when Susie was so reminiscent of Gloria. It was the way they smiled—like cats.

"Only my Christmas present." Susie smiled again, but this time her smile looked a little coy.

"And what did he say?"

"He said he'd think about it."

"He's such a push-over. Does your mom know?"

"Not yet."

"When are you going to ask her?"

"After my dad talks to her. Her first answer will be 'No,' but we can get around that."

"What the hell did you ask for?" C.C. was getting curious.

"If I tell you, it may not happen."

"Sounds more like a wish?"

"Yeah, it is."

"And are you going to tell your favorite aunt?"

"I will, when I see her later. I am babysitting tonight."

Susie made a face and dashed off to look at dresses in a window, long formal dresses that would be perfect for parties and things like that. C.C. just stood back and smiled; her niece was something else. C.C. was dying to know what she had asked Johnnie for, but she couldn't ask her directly. That would not be cool. Besides, she didn't have to. She could get it out of Johnnie much easier.

*

Norm and Buddy's date night was not going so well and this time, it was all down to him. No matter how hard he tried, Norm just couldn't get into the mood. He couldn't stop thinking about the situation at work and he was painfully aware of the cost of everything on the menu. It was one of the fancy places they had wanted to try for weeks and they made the reservation right after they first agreed to date nights, back when they still had money to throw around. Buddy looked great, too, and that just made things even worse. She had gone out and bought a new dress and had her hair and nails done. And she bought new shoes, high heeled and expensive. He had told her how good she looked, but even he could hear the tone in his voice.

As the evening went on, he knew she could tell that he wasn't into it and that just made her look worried. Knowing her, she was probably thinking that it was her—that even when she tried her best, she still wasn't good enough for him anymore. He wanted to tell her that it wasn't her, it was him. But he couldn't. Not without telling her the whole story.

He would, but not yet. He wanted to sort it out on his own and when he had another job lined up, he would mention it—casually, like it had been something he had been planning to do all along.

Instead, they struggled through the evening trying to make conversation, talking about the service, about their food, about anything to drown out the silences.

When their desserts arrived, he gave up and told her that he was tired, that it had been a long, hard week and Buddy went along with that.

"Would you like me to drive Susie home?" She offered sympathetically.

She hated driving at night and he hated that she felt she had to offer. "No, I can manage."

"I will be waiting for you," she smiled. "I bought something else that I want to show you."

*

"Hey, how is your dad doing?" Norm asked as casually as he could. They had pulled up outside Johnnie and Carol's and he had just paid Susie.

"He's fine."

"Tell him I said 'Hello.'"

She was about to get out, but turned back to look at him. "Uncle Norm?"

"Yeah?"

"Could I get your advice on something?"

"Sure?"

"I have this friend and we haven't spoken since the summer. Nothing happened, or anything, we just got busy with the new semester."

"Stuff like that happens."

"Yeah, only now everybody thinks we had a falling out—over a boy."

"Did you?"

"No. It's just now it's all awkward and every-thing."

"I see. Hey, why don't you just phone her when you get inside."

"But what if . . ."

"Don't worry about any of that. Just call her; you're still friends. Right?"

She stared at him for a moment. Then she smiled and reached out to hug his arm. "Thanks, Uncle Norm. I knew you'd understand. I guess that is why you are my favorite uncle."

That made Norm feel so much better, but half way home he remembered: he was Susie's only uncle—at least on this side of the family.

Chapter 5

"Leaving so soon?" Carol asked as she came into her kitchen. Johnnie had already filled his travel mug and was heading for the door.

"Oh, morning, Babe. Yeah. I wanted to get down to the job in Cabbagetown. They promised to have the check ready this morning, but they have been saying that for a few days."

"Is there a problem?"

"No, they said they are happy with the way everything turned out. They are just slow to pay for it, but we shouldn't worry. We know where they live."

"You're not going to go all bad-assed on them, are you?"

"Nah. She's a lawyer and he's a doctor. They're probably all ganged up."

"Did you get the deposit for the Manor Road job?"

"Yeah, but it's postdated."

"We hadn't agreed to that."

"I know, but what can I do?"

"You could search the couch for change and take me out for lunch one of these days."

"Yeah," he agreed, but didn't make eye contact. Instead he checked his watch and shrugged.

"Okay, then." She decided to let it go at that.

They both knew that there wasn't much left for him to do. The last few jobs were winding down and, other than showing his face to reassure fussy clients, all that was left was to wait for payment and that part could drag on longer than the actual project. Especially with those clients who felt entitled to try to squeeze out more than had been agreed upon.

"Okay, then," he nodded and left, leaving so many things unsaid.

She got it; he was frustrated. Dealing with clients was hard, but he really didn't help himself. It was a very competitive market and he could be so very old school about it all. He insisted that he always provided quality work and that people should be willing pay for that. That was all well and good, but it meant that they were being undercut on more and more jobs and Carol struggled to be okay with that. She had to keep reminding herself it had been one of the things she had once loved about him. Besides, they were often called in afterwards to fix the mess created by the cheaper bidders.

In the past, she had priced their quotes above the rest and for a while that had worked. Most of their business came from referrals from very contented clients for whom money was not an issue, and who enjoyed proclaiming their status by recommending "their guy." But money was tightening and the under-bidders were everywhere. She and Johnnie had talked about that, but he couldn't, or wouldn't, compromise.

"If we did lower our prices we would be stuck in a downward spiral," he'd said. "And I would rather have less, but better paid, work."

"Perhaps," she had agreed, trying not to let her growing frustrations show. "But you might have to take up golf."

"That's not a bad idea. They say there is more business done on the golf course than anywhere else."

"Sounds like old, boys club to me, but I was thinking more about how you might use all your free time."

It was one of the things he was bad at—managing his down time. That was why she was happy when he'd take off to Gloria's for a few days, now and then, through the winter. He could always find something useful to do up there and now that the kids were older, it didn't create any extra work for her. But he hadn't even mentioned going up this year. They had spent Thanksgiving with her parents, but Christmas had not yet been discussed.

Part of it was her, and part of it was him. She knew he needed time to sort his feelings out after his father had died. She could understand that, but what she really wanted to do was to reach in and shake him out of it. What Jake had asked him to do was just plain wrong. It just wasn't who Johnnie was.

She still got angry whenever she thought about it and she couldn't talk with him about it. How could she? "I think your dead father was very selfish in asking you to assist in his suicide."

Instead, and maybe for her own selfish reasons, she had decided to slap an embargo on his entire family. She felt she had to, and she felt it was for his own good. He said he understood and agreed to go along with it, but the secret calls and texts with his sisters soon became obvious. Carol was annoyed by that. She couldn't help but see it as a test of his loyalty; a tug-of-war between her and his family.

As soon as she realized that she was thinking like that, she had to reach inside of herself and give herself a good shaking. If she couldn't trust Johnnie to do the

right thing—after all they had been through together—well, that would just be far too Mary-like.

Poor Mary; how was she coping with it all now
that everyone knew about C.C.?

And then to have the man she had vilified for
years come back and make peace with them all. How
the hell was she ever going to be able to show her face
again?

Carol couldn't help but feel sorry for her mother-
in-law, despite all the harm her hysterics and antics
had caused through the years. Not so much with her
and Johnnie, more so with Buddy and Norm, and with
C.C., though she would never admit it.

She and Johnnie had not discussed that part of it,
but one of the reasons she wanted them to keep their
distance for a while was to give Mary some time to try
to redeem herself. After all those years of self-righteousness, she must be burning with shame. Carol
had thought about calling her, but couldn't think how
she could step around all that had happened. Besides,
Gloria was more than capable of looking after her and
she would let them know if there were any problems.

Except that, Gloria wasn't getting any younger
and Carol really missed the old lady. They all did,
Johnnie, Joey, and especially Susie; she and Gloria
had some kind of strange bond. But Carol couldn't see
any way she could back down—and not for the sake of
her own ego. She was trying to send a message to his
family: Stop talking Johnnie for granted.

It was well-intentioned, but she had begun to wonder: In trying to keep them away, was she creating the
divide between herself and Johnnie?

Family was everything to him and had been since
they first got together. He had always been very pro-
tective of them—and hyper sensitive to any criticism

coming from outsiders. She had always been able to navigate her way through that before, but now things felt different. Now it felt like he was starting to look at her as an outsider and that was something she never felt before.

And it wasn't just because work was drying up, even though being able to work and provide for his family meant everything to Johnnie. It was how he defined himself.

And it wasn't just that the guy who always fixed his family's problem could not help his father out in the end. There was something else. It was like he had started second-guessing everything; even them.

She shook her head to clear her mind for the day ahead. The kids had left for school, too. They had insisted that they wanted to walk and Carol had let it go at that. They were up to something and they probably needed to talk in private. She wasn't worried. If they got themselves into a mess, she and Johnnie would be able to sort it out. Besides, the winter hadn't really hit Toronto, yet. It was getting closer, drifting south by the day, but it was still not too bad and the kids liked to walk.

She poured another coffee and went into her home office—a large room that Johnnie had fitted out to what he thought were her exact requirements. He had even built her a roll top desk. It didn't really work with her laptop sitting on top, but . . .

She scanned through her emails, but there was little of immediate importance. She had sent out quotes and had a few polite replies that they were being considered. But one message caught her eye. It was from Ben Davies, the man with the "Cinema Project." He wanted to continue their recent discussion and asked if she might be free to meet him for lunch. He had suggested Scaramouche, too.

*

As soon as she walked in, he rose to greet her and she was glad she had taken the time to dress up a bit. He was charming and handsome, and he even held her chair as she sat. That almost flustered her.

"I am so glad you could come," he said when she was settled. "And at such short notice. Would you care for some wine?"

He held the bottle over her glass and waited for her response. "Please," she agreed and noticed his manicured nails. Johnnie's were always frayed and usually stained with varnish or paint.

"I have to tell you that I was very impressed by you during our previous discussion." Ben began as he poured the deep red wine into her glass. "And I felt that we might have much more to talk about."

She sipped from her wine before answering. It was rich and the aroma was so appealing. It was probably very expensive. "Such as?"

"Well. Let's order first and then we can talk."

He had barely motioned when the waiter arrived. They both decided on the Mushroom Pasta and laughed about that. "Great minds . . ." Ben joked and then raised his glass. "To exploring new possibilities."

Carol raised hers, but said nothing. She wasn't sure what she was getting herself into. She had told herself that it would be a business lunch but now that she was here, it didn't feel like that. Ben flashed a smile and waited for her to respond. He had perfect teeth and was so clean-shaven that she was almost tempted to reach out and touch his cheek. In the winter, Johnnie only shaved on weekends.

After they finished their appetizers, Ben topped up their glasses. "You know I have more in mind than just refurbishing the cinema?"

"Oh?"

"Yes. I want to restore the whole building."

"Including the dry cleaners and the convenience store?" Carol asked as she tried to figure out what he was really talking about. "Will they have to go?"

"Yes. They have been long term lessees, but we cannot let things like that get in the way."

"Nothing can stand in the way of progress?"

He paused to look at her for a moment. He seemed to be able to see more than she wanted him to see. She was a little uncomfortable in his gaze, and a little titillated.

"I don't see it that way."

"How do you see it?"

"I see it that I am going to restore a queen to her former, and deserved glory. She was a much-celebrated example of the best of Art Deco when she opened. Since then, she has been treated so poorly; it is not what she deserves. Is it progress to restore such a beauty to what she was?"

Carol didn't respond, she didn't trust what might have come out of her mouth. A part of her thought it was all a bit cheesy—if she was reading the situation correctly. But there was another part of her that was enjoying every moment. Perhaps it was the wine, or perhaps it was eating some place where the food came on plates and wasn't wrapped in paper on plastic serving trays. Or, perhaps, she was just annoyed at Johnnie. He had all the time in the world to listen to his sisters' problems but when she needed to talk to him . . .

"Maybe you think I am being foolish?" Ben asked after the waiter had left their main courses and blended back into the backdrop.

"I haven't decided what to think, yet."

"Then let me say some more." He spoke with eagerness, but waited for her to nod. "When we talked at our last meeting, I got the sense that you might be the type of person that I could form an understanding with. I got the sense that you could see the value in restoring life to where it should have been."

He paused to gauge her reaction, but continued before she had to say anything. "Owing to a series of events in my life, I have become the type of man who looks at the world and gets annoyed by all the compromises we are obliged to make. I have become the type of man who believes that we only live once and, even then, we do not get to live forever. I have also come to believe that we should celebrate this existence that too many of us take for granted. And that we should always make bold and brazen statements in everything we do."

He paused again for her reaction, but she didn't offer any. He wasn't the person she had first assumed. At their previous meeting she had seen him as a man in a grey suit with spreadsheets and graphs; the type of man she would have passed in the street. Now he had such color and vibrancy in an old, corny movie kind of way.

"That is why I am going to restore the old restaurant that was there. That is why I am going to refit the theatre to accommodate live performance as well as screenings. That is why I am going to remake The

Royale to the queen that she once was; the queen of sophisticated night life."

He paused to sip his wine and Carol felt obliged to speak. "And how is all of this to be financed?" It was very gauche of her, but he was getting a bit carried away with it all.

"Ah, you have a practical mind. I had hoped so. Financing will not be a major concern. By virtue of my family's involvement in land and property speculation over the last few decades, I have access to the means to undo some of the damage they caused."

"And how will your family feel about that?"

"My father is dead, my mother is in the later stages of Alzheimer's, and I have no siblings. I am unencumbered in that regard.

"Are you married?" She heard herself ask.

"Ah, the marriage question."

"Sorry, it isn't any of my business," Carol stammered a little. She hadn't meant to ask. It just popped out.

"I was married, but the former Mrs. Davies and I have gone our separate and irreconcilable ways."

"I'm sorry to hear that."

"Don't be. We were never really happy together and after ten years of avoiding that, we were finally forced to come to our senses. While we had begun in what we once believed was love, we found ourselves living unhappily ever after in a constant state of compromise."

"Did you have children?"

"One. A beautiful young lady . . ." He stopped abruptly and looked down at his plate. "She is no longer with us," he continued in a voice that was tinged with sadness. "She developed leukemia and, as hard as she tried, she couldn't defeat it."

"Oh, I am so sorry." Carol wished she hadn't asked, and she wished she could reach out and touch the back of Ben's hand.

"Thank you. But if anything, it was her short life that became my inspiration."

"What was her name?"

"Her name, and forgive me if I sound pedantic, is Melanie. While she is no longer with me in the outside world, she will always remain in the very core of what I am."

Carol smiled and nodded as sympathetically as she could. Burying a child was the most terrifying thing she could imagine.

"Or," Ben corrected himself. "What I am striving to become. After Melanie passed, I could no longer find any satisfaction working in the high offices on Bay Street—I was a financial advisor to a very wealthy client base. I had once loved that life and all the trappings, but losing something so precious made me realize how vain and worthless it really was."

He paused to sip from his glass as there was a touch of hoarseness in his voice. "And it brought matters between me and Melanie's mother into sharp focus. Naturally, grief was a factor and we could never expect to see a day that would not have a shadow over it." He paused and sipped from his glass again like he was reconsidering what he had just said.

"Perhaps a happier couple could have faced it. Or a couple with other children, but we couldn't. In fact, I now believe that it was only Melanie's battle that kept us together. And when it was over, there was nothing but sadness and regret between us."

They finished their meals in relative silence, only commenting on the delicate and harmonious blending of tastes on their plates; combinations that might not have seemed so obvious at first, but that now came together in an unexpected harmony. A harmony that was perfectly complimented by the second bottle of a wine—another subtle vintage with an intoxicating aroma.

They agreed on desserts, too. Something sweet to savor while they began to talk of possibilities, and practicalities, and pitfalls. They ordered coffees, too. Short, bitter espressos to brace them for when they would step back into the cold reality of the world outside.

Chapter 6

"I would like to return this dress," Buddy mumbled to the elegant young man who was standing behind the counter. He had watched her come in, hesitate for a moment, and almost leave before she had finally managed to drum up the courage to approach him.

"I am sorry?" He answered with a quizzical look on his face.

"I just want to return this dress," Buddy repeated with as much conviction as she could muster. She tried to make it sound like she had simply changed her mind about her purchase, but it felt like she was lowering the flag and surrendering the last of her pride—and any hopes she had of salvaging her relationship with Norm.

She had to face up to it. It had been so naive of her to have imagined things could have turned out any other way. A fancy dress was never going to change all that had happened between them. They had tried to revive their relationship, but the damage had been fatal. All that was left for them to do now was to linger in the neverland that couples with young children moved into after their love had withered and died; lingering for the sake of the children. She handed over the bag containing the box the dress came in. "And here is the receipt. I removed the labels, but they are still in the box."

"Very well, Madam," the young cashier agreed and took the bag, opened the box and read the receipt. Then her looked directly into her face like he was genuinely curious. "Was there a problem with the dress?"

"Not with the dress," Buddy answered without thinking and quickly turned her head. She hadn't wanted to get into a conversation about it. What could she say? The dress was perfect. It fit so well and it felt so great on. It made her look the way she had wanted to, but . . . sadly, it was all too little, too late. "I just wish to return it," she repeated and tried to stare him down.

"I see," the young man offered in a more conciliatory tone as he lowered his gaze. "And would Madam care to try something else? Perhaps something more . . ."

Buddy shook her head. She had tears in the corner of her eyes. "No, thank you. I just want to return it."

There was no way she could explain it to him. He was young and very dashing and he had his whole life ahead of him. When life was not going the way he wanted, he could simply go to the store and pick out something new. Sure, he had probably known some heartbreak, but he hadn't paid the price yet. At least not the price that she had paid.

"I see," he repeated and looked up at her again. "I am sorry, but I cannot offer you a refund. It's company policy," he added and nodded his head towards the back of the store. "But I can give you a full store credit."

She might have told him that was of no use to her. That there was nothing in the store that she would ever want again. But she didn't, she just nodded her head.

He noticed, and slowly turned towards the computer on the counter. He began to tap on the screen and waited, then tapped some more, each tap sounding like the ticking of a clock. "This will only take a few minutes," he told her. "Are you sure you wouldn't care to take a look around while you are waiting?"

He paused for her reaction, but she didn't offer one. "We have some wonderful new Christmas outfits over there," he continued. "They would be perfect for family get-togethers, or office parties."

Before Buddy could control herself, she began to cry. Softly and almost silently, like the way snow melted. He looked up at her and his eyes grew wider. He had deep, brown eyes. He had long, black eyelashes. His perfect face froze for a moment as he began to realize.

"Oh, sistren," he exclaimed and raised his hand to his cheek. "I am so sorry."

He reached out with his other hand. He had long fingers with perfectly trimmed nails. He wore a ring on every finger. "That was so insensitive of me." He stepped out from behind the counter and walked towards her with his arms stretched out, invitingly.

Without even thinking about it, Buddy nestled in against him, turning her head to rest against his shoulder and coming face to face with their reflection in a long mirror. He was so tall and slender, and he was dressed from the pages of the store's men's catalogue—the high-priced fashion that she couldn't even get Norm to look at, let alone consider wearing.

She couldn't help herself. She stood staring at their reflection. It was such an odd thing to see. This tall and slender young man who looked like one of the mannequins in the window was holding her, a sad, frumpy looking woman in a tired old coat that sagged, almost to her knees.

"Oh, sistren," he repeated. "I am so sorry. I should have realized."

Buddy pulled away and reached into her pocket for a tissue. Her nose was running and she didn't want to snotter all over his tight, embroidered jacket.

"Is it that obvious?" she blurted out as she wiped at her nose and her eyes.

The poor young man looked even more flustered and held her at arm's length. "No, but . . ."

"It's okay to be honest. In fact, it would be a refreshing change."

"Was it a man?"

"Yes, and no."

"It's always a man, sistren. Don't go blaming yourself. Men don't deserve people like us."

Buddy had to laugh at that, a nervous, giggly laugh. "No, they don't."

Then she thought about what he had just said. "Are you . . ." she began to ask and stammered.

"Gay? You better believe it, sistren. As queer as they come, and my name is Jerome."

"I'm Buddy."

"Buddy?"

"It's from Rosemary, you know? Rosemary . . . Rosebud . . . Buddy!"

"Oh, you white people and your made-up names."

They were still laughing at that when a tall, thin young woman came out from the back of the store. She made a point of looking Buddy up and down, wrinkled her nose, shrugged, and then quickly rearranged her face to smile at Jerome. "Is everything okay?"

"Everything is cool, C.D.V. I'm just rapping with my new best friend."

"Oh? I see. Well I am here now if you want to take your break."

"Sure," Jerome agreed. "I just have to finish Buddy's credit."

"Buddy?"

"Yeah, you know, Rosemary, Rosebud, Buddy."

"Oh. How . . . quaint." The tall, thin young woman shrugged and went off to rearrange the dresses on one of the racks. She too was dressed from the catalogue and also looked like a mannequin, tall and slender. She stood perfectly straight in her high-heels and moved hangers in and out without even scratching her long, brightly colored nails. She was everything Buddy resented in younger women.

Jerome came back from behind the counter and handed Buddy the credit note. He did it with such flourish that she had to smile.

"Thank you, Jerome. You have been so kind."

She turned and walked towards the door, hoping he might say something else. She wasn't ready to be on her own just yet.

"Buddy?" he called after her. "I'm going to the coffee shop across the street. Would you like to come with me? We can have cappuccinos and 'dis' this man that broke your heart."

*

For no other reason than she was feeling so terribly alone and afraid, Buddy spilled her entire life story to Jerome. He had gotten them refills and had texted the tall, thin young woman to tell her that he was taking his lunch break early. Then he had listened intently and had smiled encouragingly when Buddy wavered. But when she came to the part about her date night, his eyes grew wider and softer.

"And now, I have gone and lost him," Buddy added, as if in conclusion. "And the worst part is that it should happen now after I tried so hard to change."

"Rosebud," Jerome responded and took her dry, cold hands in his. They were so warm and soft. "Whether or not you have lost him, and there is nothing in what you have told me to suggest that you have—that is no reason to give up on yourself. You just spent all of this time telling me about how unhappy you were with the way things were. Why would you ever even consider going back to that?"

"How can you say; 'Whether or not you have lost him,' after what I told you?"

"You told me that your date night didn't go well, but even you don't know why that is."

"It's obvious; it is because he has had enough of me and can't take it anymore."

"It is not obvious to me, and that doesn't make any sense."

"Why do you say that?"

"Because there is something else that is obvious. If a man was going to dump someone who had behaved the way you say you did, he would have done it a long time ago. Maybe you were not nearly as bad as you think you were."

"Thanks for saying that," she laughed, despite herself. "But you have no idea what I was like. I can say it now; I was a totally self-centered, selfish bitch."

"We can all be self-centered little bitches from time to time, but you have moved past all of that now. Right?"

It was more than a platitude. This young man that she had just met was looking at her like he really wanted to believe in her. And not because he was just being nice. There was something very deep and genuine about him.

"How can you be so sure? I know I'm not."

"Because I have seen all of this kind of thing before."

"Really?"

"Yeah, really. When I was still a mixed-up kid—back in Jamaica, my mother had this really bad problem with pills and booze and every time she got herself into a mess, she would swear that she was done with it all—only she wasn't."

As he spoke, Buddy noticed the change in his voice. He no longer used the clipped, polished words he had enunciated so precisely when he first spoke to her. Now he began to drawl and she could hear his soft, warm accent. And there was something else. His face had become calm and impassive. It was like he was talking about something that had happened to someone else. It was like it wasn't personal for him anymore.

"Then one day," he continued and became a little more animated. "She sat me down at the kitchen table and looked into my eyes. She told me that she wanted to change her life and that this time she really was going to do it. She said that she had already gone to a few meetings and they had changed the way she looked at everything."

He paused for a moment to gauge Buddy's reaction and then smiled, as if to himself.

"And even though I had heard her say things like that a hundred times before, I knew that this time she was telling me the truth. I knew it because I could see it in her eyes. She had the same look that I see on your face."

"Did she make it?"

"She's been clean and sober for almost eleven years. And she was there for me when I came out."

"That is wonderful. Not everyone gets that type of support."

"She is a Jamaican Mammy; they love their sons no matter what. And the best part is that every day she makes it, it reminds me that we have to go on believing that good things will happen—even to people who are all messed up. All any of us has is to really try and not give up trying when things go bad."

"I hope you are right. I just can't imagine what I would do if . . . well, you know."

"I know, Rosebud, but there is something you are not looking at here. There could be a whole heap of reasons why your man wasn't what you needed him to be that night. He could be going through stuff of his own."

"But why wouldn't he just tell me?" But even as she said it, she realized how foolish that was. She had never been the type of wife that Norm could take his troubles to.

Jerome watched her closely and gently squeezed her hands. "Don't go blaming yourself for that, either. Sometimes men just can't talk about the things that are really bothering them. They all have to go through that strong, silent, macho thing first. Maybe he just needs to go out drinking beer with one of his friends. That's when men really open up about their stuff."

"But what else could it be?"

"It could be anything. His sports team could be losing. Or he could have gone out and bought himself a big, bad motorcycle and hasn't figured out how to tell you about it. You know the way men are. Just send him out to have a boys' night with his friends. After that, he will have worked it out—or he will tell you about it. You'll see."

He smiled and squeezed her hands again. Then he abruptly let go and reached for his phone. He checked the text and laughed. "I have to go. Cruella De Vil is waiting to have her lunch."

"That's not a nice thing to call her."

"She doesn't mind. I think she even likes it, and I think it suits her." He laughed again and hugged her tight. "Hang in there, Rosebud. Your time to bloom is just around the corner."

She was still smiling at that as she made her way out of the coffee shop. The wind had picked up and, for a moment, she wished she had brought the car. She thought about hailing a cab, but the walk would do her good. Jerome had given her so much to think about. So much that she decided to walk all the way to St Clair, even though it was uphill. She bundled up and put her head down.

She really wanted to believe that Jerome was right. She really wanted to believe that good things happened when you tried to change, but her head was full of little voices that tried so hard to dissuade her. Little voices that tried to remind her of all the times she had been hurt; of all the times she had given so much and gotten so little back, and of all the times when she had tried to do what was right and had it thrown back in her face.

Neural networks, she reminded herself.

She had to stop listening to those voices. They were the reasons she had gotten lost before. Those voices never had anything nice to say about anybody and even though they sounded warm and comforting, all they ever told her to do was to feel sorry for her-self.

What was most annoying about that was, despite everything she had managed to change, they had never really gone away. They were always lurking somewhere in her mind, always ready to burble up when things didn't go the way she wanted. But now, she knew better. Sure, there would be set-backs, but that wasn't going to stop her. She was going to pick herself up, dust herself off, and start all over again.

Despite the cold, she was feeling so much better as she made her way up Avenue Road.

Jerome was right; it could have been anything. Norm had not been indifferent to her; he had just been preoccupied by something else. If anything, she should be feeling bad for not being there for him. But she couldn't allow herself to think like that, either. Damn, this changing business was so hard.

She began thinking of all the ways she might casually get Norm to open up when she passed Scaramouche and stopped dead in her tracks. Carol had just come out with a very handsome and dapper man. He hailed her a cab and kissed her on both cheeks before she got in. He even waved after her as it drove away.

Without thinking, Buddy pulled out her phone and called Johnnie.

"What's up?"

Buddy hesitated until he asked again and then blurted out the first thing that came to her mind.

"I just had coffee with a very dapper young Jamaican gentleman."

She cursed herself. She should have said it was a pocket dial.

"Does Norm know about this?" He was joking, but she still felt like she had to explain.

"Don't be silly, he's gay."

"Really? I never would have figured you for a fag hag."

Chapter 7

Because she had enjoyed having a laugh about that, Buddy wanted to get together for coffee. Johnnie wasn't too keen on it, but he was also at loose ends and had nothing better to do. He had just spent most of the afternoon hanging around a Home Depot, not far from Buddy's subway stop.

He wasn't really in the mood for company, but there was something in his sister's voice. It reminded him of when they were kids and she had something she could only say to him. He could never say no to her when she was like that so he agreed to head over and pick her up. Besides, he had been up and down every aisle, twice, and there was nothing left that he could even pretend to be interested in. Having nothing to do was killing him.

He had visited each one of the jobs earlier and there was no excuse to go back. Everything was clicking along nicely and he knew better than to hang around. It would have made it seem like he didn't trust his guys. He did; they were the best and they had earned the right to be allowed do their work without the boss standing over them.

He understood the way guys like that thought. They came in and did what they were asked to do without whining and complaining. They always gave their best because they knew that was expected of them. And he liked to pay them over and above—another one of the things Carol said was going to have to be reviewed.

He went outside and got into his truck. After it roared to life, he flicked on the wipers for a moment. There had been a brief flurry and his windshield was covered in snow dust. He carefully backed out through the maze of abandoned trolleys and carts and slowly pulled out of the carpark.

The coming year was looking bleak. Normally by now, Carol would have four of five jobs on the schedule. This year, they had one. It was a good one—a total tear down and rebuild on Manor Road. He would get at least three months out of it, but after that . . .

There was no way of denying it; things were getting tight, and they were going to get a lot tighter. When interest rates were lower, everyone could cash in on their line-of-credit, or remortgage. House prices in Toronto were still climbing so it made sense. But rates would have to rise and then it was only a matter of time before house prices began to drop off. He had seen it all before.

He and Carol would not be too badly affected—in the short term. They managed to pay off their mortgage early, and they had been able to stash money here and there. Carol crunched the numbers and said they could ride out a few dry months, eight to ten, if they had to. "Beyond that," she laughed, "we might have to start selling our bodies—or at least a few organs, or something."

He wasn't worried about the money side of things; they would find a way. What was really bothering him was the growing sense that guys like him were becoming obsolete. Quality tradesmen were a dying breed. The guys he had worked with—before he went out on his own—had all jacked it in and gone on to do other things. "The last of the dinosaurs," they used to call him whenever they met up.

Back then, he scoffed at them and told them that they just weren't able to hack it. But now, there were so many times when his own words came back to him and he sounded like he was a little boy whistling in the graveyard—a graveyard full of master carpenters, brick layers, stone masons, plasters and plumbers. Nobody wanted them anymore, not when they could get some grunter for half the price; some grunter who barely knew which end of a hammer to use.

Last winter, when he was working on the boat house at the cottage, he and Gloria had talked about all of that. She had listened sympathetically and then smiled. "Always remember," she had told him with a twinkle in her eye. "There will always be a place for you here."

"Doing what?" he had asked.

"Sitting on the deck opposite me."

He sighed softly as he pulled up near the subway entrance. There was no parking, but he could 'stand' until the parking guy showed up and moved him on. He missed Gloria and his winter trips to the cottage. There was nothing better than hauling lumber back up the snowy track and working out in the cold. It made him feel so Canadian. And he could always find something to do. The old place was in need of constant care.

He was overdue a visit, but he wasn't sure how to approach Carol on it. She was right about his family. He needed a break from them and they needed to get on with their lives without dragging him into every little thing that happened.

Even as he thought that, he looked at himself in the mirror. He was the biggest part of the problem. When it came to his sisters—and his mother—he could be the biggest suck of all. And, as if on cue, Buddy emerged from the subway, saw the truck and waved. Dutifully he drove forward to let her in.

*

Buddy was still very excited about her chat with the guy in the store and insisted on getting the coffees, and a half dozen donuts. She took one and pushed the others towards him. She obviously had a favor to ask of him, but he bit into one anyway.

That was another one of the things Carol had said to him, recently. He was getting soft around the middle and should lay off the donuts for a while—at least until he was able to work them off again. She had probably meant it as a joke but lately, she seemed to be taking a lot of little shots at him.

"So?" he asked. It was obvious that Buddy wanted him to force her to tell him about whatever it was that she wanted to talk about. It was a game they had played for years.

"What do you mean? Can't I even have coffee with you, anymore?"

"Coffee, yeah, but you only buy me donuts when you need a favor."

"That's not true."

"Sure, it is."

"I buy you donuts all the time."

"And you ask me for a favor every time."

"No, I don't."

"Okay, you don't." He picked up another crueller and bit into it, showering the stubble on his chin with sugary crumbs. "How are Norm and the kids?"

"The kids are doing fine, thanks. Adjusting to the new school year, and all of that."

"And Norm?"

She didn't respond immediately, so he had his answer.

"What's he done now?"

"It's not like that."

"So, what's the issue, then?"

"Maybe there is no issue. Maybe it's just all in my head."

"Then it's still an issue."

"Maybe, but it's not like before. I have changed, you know."

"So, are you telling me you have a new issue?"

She sipped her coffee as she weighed her options. They both knew that she had to talk about it. The only question was: how was she was going to talk about it?

He could see that she had changed—in a way. Now, instead of always being the tragic victim in everything that had happened between her and Norm, she had become the perpetrator. It didn't strike him as a very positive development, but at least he could honestly tell her that she had changed when she asked—and she would ask.

And there was something else that had changed. Since their mother had gone to live with Gloria, Buddy was feeling isolated and was now turning to Johnnie whenever she needed reassurance.

Carol was right about so many things. His family were all the same; needy and selfish, and totally oblivious to anything anybody around them might be going through. They had always been like that and, over the years, he had learned to go along with it all. He had never been able to tell them when he was upset and, of course, he hadn't said anything about what their father had asked him to do.

He ate another crueller as he waited. He would hear her out, but he was going to force her to come out and say it. She was still pretending to be deep in her own thoughts, but she looked over at him every now and then.

"Okay, okay," she finally decided. "I will tell you."

And she did. She told him about every little thing she had gone through since their father had died; all of her efforts to change, and how well she and Norm had been getting along—stuff she had already shared with him so many times on the phone.

Still, Johnnie sat through it all and waited. Whatever was coming was something that had to be said face-to-face. He had finished his coffee and wanted to get up and get another one, but he didn't want to interrupt her.

Then she told him all about their date night and before he could offer any comment, she told him everything she and Jerome had talked about. "He made it all seem so simple and so clear," she said like she was sharing an epiphany. "I was worried that it was something I had done when clearly it is something going on with Norm."

"Has this Jerome guy even met Norm?"

"I doubt it. Why do you ask?"

"Never mind. So, are you going to sit down and talk about it with Norm?"

"Do you think I should?"

"Yeah."

"But what if it is something that he is not ready to talk about?"

"Then you might have to wait until he is ready."

He raised his empty cup and looked inside. She noticed and rose immediately.

"Let me get some more."

She took both their cups and rushed over to the counter. He sat and watched her. Despite his frustrations, he had to smile. This Jerome guy had really fired her up. Johnnie had not seen her like this in years and that was good to see. She was a pain in his ass, but she was still his sister.

She came back with their refills and a box of Timbits. "These are for the kids, but I am sure they won't mind if you take a few."

He did. He popped one in his mouth and smiled. "So, you want me to talk with Norm?"

"Would you? Only don't make a big deal out of it. Just mention it casually the next time you guys are hanging out."

"Norm and I haven't seen each other since the summer."

"You guys haven't had a falling-out, have you?"

"Not that I know of."

"Is it because of Carol? I know she doesn't want you to be so involved with your family, anymore, but she can't mean Norm, too?"

He thought about saying something about that. About how that wasn't the way things were, but what was the point? Buddy was going to see things her way no matter what he said. Besides, Carol was more than able to fight her own battles and didn't need him running interference for her.

"Okay," he agreed and popped another Timbit in his mouth. "Tell Norm to give me a call."

"Could you not call him? It would seem . . . well more like the way things used to be."

"He was the one who always called me."

"Then it might be nice for you to call him instead, and leave some for the kids."

"Okay, okay. When do you want me to call him?"

"Let a few days go by so it doesn't seem like a setup."

"And what would you like me to say to him?"

"Really, Johnnie? Do I have to tell you what to say?"

"It might be better."

"Why are you being like this?"

"Like what?"

"Never mind."

She checked her watch and rose in a flurry. "I have to run. The kids will be getting out of school in a few minutes."

"Come on," Johnnie said after he had drained his cup. "I'll drive you over."

"That would be so nice. The kids will be thrilled to see you. You are their favorite uncle."

"I am their only uncle—on this side."

*

After he had dropped Buddy and the kids off, Johnnie headed for home.

He had turned it over and over in his mind and there was no upside. He had to reach out to Norm— for Buddy's sake—and in doing so he was going to risk pissing Carol off, big time. But then again, everything he did these days seemed to piss her off.

He had missed Norm and he might be able to pass it off as just the two of them going for a few beers together—just to catch up. Carol was okay with Norm but as she had reminded Johnnie more than a few times, Norm and Buddy needed all the time they could get to try to sort themselves out.

It did make sense, but it also felt like Carol was calling all the shots these days.

He knew a lot of that came down to the fact that he had nothing to do. If he was busy, he would feel better about everything. He would feel like he and Carol were a real partnership against the world. Now, he just felt like . . .

He wouldn't let himself think about that. Instead, he tried to laugh it off. He was, he decided, just suffering from some kind of slow-season mood disorder. Medical science hadn't figured it out yet, but it was very common among construction contractors and those who worked outside. He made himself laugh at that, but it was a hollow laugh. Things were different. He was different.

The way his father had died had really messed him up inside. He couldn't stop thinking about it and every time he did, he thought of a different 'what-if.' And every time he did, he ended up with the same, sad realization: he just wasn't the man he had always thought he was.

He knew that Carol had some idea what he was going through, and he also knew that she knew he wasn't ready to talk about it. How could he? He was feeling bad enough without going back and digging all of that up.

He often thought about talking to Gloria about it, but he would have to do it face-to-face. With his mother there, that would be difficult even if he could just swing a few days up there.

Shit. His life had gotten so messed up.

He pulled up in his driveway, but before he got out, he looked at himself in the mirror and tried to look like Michael Corleone.

Just when I thought I was out, they pull me back in, he told his reflection.

It just smiled back at him, knowingly.

Chapter 8

It was another cold, windy morning and Susie had her fur-lined hood up. She needed to feel secure even if it meant that she could not see on either side, but she could hear Joey walking along behind her. He had borrowed a pair of their dad's work boots and hadn't tied the laces. He had just stuffed them in so the boots were loose and sounded like they were clomping along on their own. And he had his hands pushed deep into his pockets so that he walked with his shoulders hunched.

He was wearing his dad's black and red mackinaw—the padded one that was way too big for him. He wore it unbuttoned over his old, grey waffle sweatshirt. He hadn't showered in a few days and was also wearing one of his dad's big belts, but at least it kept his pants hitched up.

"Did Mom see you leaving the house like that?"

"Obviously."

"And she didn't say anything?"

"She did."

"What did she say?"

"Who cares."

Susie was a bit shocked by that, but she just nodded. Joey was in one of his moods, again.

Things had been getting very tense at home, mostly between her brother and her parents. It seemed to Susie that not a day went by without him doing something to make them angry. And, it seemed to her like he was doing some of it deliberately.

She had overheard her mom and dad talk about him a few times. They both said that they were starting to become concerned about his attitude, but they had decided not to react for now.

Susie also overheard them say that he was probably just going through a phase, but she was worried. She had only ever known her brother to be bright and warm. This dark, brooding side of him was scary. He had become so surly and stayed in his room for hours with his headphones on. Sometimes she was afraid to even go in and try talking with him.

She thought she got it. He was almost two years older than her so she couldn't expect to really understand everything he was going through. He was sixteen and most of the kids in grade eleven were going through things at home, and most of them were behaving and dressing like they were trying to prove a point.

"Did you talk to Dad this morning?"

"No."

"Neither did I, he left early."

Joey didn't say anything about that so they walked in silence for a while, a silence that was punctuated only by the clump, clump, clump of their father's work boots. That just made things worse for Susie. Her family didn't talk the way they used to. It was like each one of them had gone off into rooms inside of themselves and closed their doors and she needed to talk with someone.

There were so many things she needed to talk about. It frightened her that her dad had just lost his dad and everybody had just gone on like nothing had happened. Her dad said he was okay with it, but Susie could see that he wasn't. She had tried talking with him about all of that, but he wouldn't. Instead, he'd just change the subject.

She needed to talk with her mom, too. Her mom had always been the one who had made them all sit down together and deal with their issues, but now she seemed to have given up on that. She was always busy with something else, and she was worried about something. She pretended she wasn't, but Susie could tell.

"What should I do?" Susie had asked Gloria one evening when she was feeling particularly cut off from everything and just needed to hear a warm and friendly voice.

Her great grandmother had listened while Susie had poured her heart out. But Gloria did it without offering her usual advice and reassurances and that was the most unsettling thing of all. Before, Susie had always been able to count on her.

"People just need time to get over things like this," Gloria had finally answered. "Death affects people in different ways and everyone needs to deal with it in their own way."

She had gone on to tell Susie that everything would be alright, but it just felt like coddling and that was something Susie was beginning to outgrow. She was frightened and confused and she needed real answers.

*

"Are you mad at me about something?" she asked Joey when their silence had stretched on far too long.

"No."

"Are you sure?"

He didn't even respond, so she turned her head to look at him. He had a pained expression on his face.

"Are you sure?" she repeated and waited for him to answer.

He didn't. He just walked right past her.

She wanted to chase after him and make him turn around and tell her what the matter was. She wanted to force her father to sit down and explain why he was becoming so distant, and she wanted to make her mother talk with her and to tell her that everything would be okay. But she couldn't.

Instead, she walked off on her own to where her friends met every morning before school.

*

"Then I waited for him at recess," Susie told C.C. later that evening.

After another strained dinner with her family, Susie had quietly wandered off to her room. She needed to talk to someone and she needed to do it privately. And she had called her aunt because she was the only one who seemed to be able to find the time to really listen to her.

"But he never came out. I asked some of his friends if they had seen him, and do you know what they told me? Joey wasn't even at school, today. And they told me that he had been suspended."

"Oh dear," C.C. responded, but she didn't sound as shocked as Susie would have expected. It almost sounded like C.C. thought it was funny. "That doesn't sound like our little Joey."

"No, and I am so worried."

"I don't think you should be. Stuff like this happens all the time. Do you happen to know why he got suspended?"

"I heard that he got into an argument with one of his teachers."

"Oh dear. Which one?"

"His Cultural Studies teacher."

"Oh, I wouldn't worry too much about that. After all, based on everything I have read recently, I think that is what Cultural Studies is supposed to be about."

"What do you mean, C.C.?" Susie was getting confused. She couldn't be sure if her aunt was not taking her seriously, or if she was trying to redirect her.

"What I mean, Susie, is that courses like this are all part of the whole political-correctness fad. They are about teaching kids what they are supposed to be offended by. I really think it would be better if they taught you guys how to run a profitable lemonade stand, instead."

"But this is serious, C.C., he has been suspended. What am I supposed to tell Mom and Dad?"

"Maybe it's not for you to tell them."

"But I have to."

"And why do you think you have to?"

"Because I know about it and I wouldn't want them to think I kept it from them."

"I see. Susie, you know that keeping things to yourself is a big part of what being in a family is really about. Especially when those things are about other people. I don't think you should say anything to your parents about any of this—at least not for now. It is Joey's business and he will tell them when he is good and ready."

"Are you sure?"

"Of course not. How can anybody be sure of anything in our family? But my point is that it is for Joey to tell and even if he doesn't, your parents will find out anyway."

"But that will make everything worse than it already is."

"It might, or it might make things better. Sometimes, when people get lost in their own heads, having to deal with other peoples' problems is often the very thing they need to draw them out again."

"But you don't understand, C.C.. I have never seen my parents like this before."

"I do understand, Susie. I understand far more than you realize. Don't forget, I used to be the troubled teenager in my family. I'm sure you have heard all of the terrible stories."

Susie knew she was supposed to laugh at that, but she couldn't.

"Susie," C.C. continued when she didn't. "I don't mean to sound like some old condescending know-it-all, but what you have to remember is that you have never seen your father having to deal with the death of his father before. And in this particular situation, he is having to deal with the death of someone who hadn't been around in years. That kind of thing leaves all sorts of unresolved issues. But trust me, Susie. This is all just a part of life. It may all seem new and frightening to you, but it's just another one of those things we all have to get through."

"But I just want to find a way to make things better for everybody."

"Me too, Susie, but sometimes you have to wait until the time is right and not go charging in with a solution that nobody is ready for. Trust me, I just happen to be an expert in things like that."

"Do you think they will ever be ready?"

"Susie! You know better than that. You know your mother and father, and you know your brother. They are all really good people who are just dealing with the crap life has thrown at them."

"But they are all acting so different now."

"Stuff like this has been going on all the time. The only difference is that you are older now, and you are more observant—perhaps a bit too observant. All of these things have happened before, but you were too young to notice."

"Joey never got suspended before."

"That's true, but your father did."

"Really?"

"Yes. When he was back in high school. I was still a little kid then and I wasn't supposed to know about it, but Buddy told me that he put a potato in the principal's tail-pipe."

"Why?"

"Who knows? Your daddy was what used to be called 'a very high-spirited young man' in those days. Your poor grandmother was so concerned that he was acting out over not having his father around, but I think he was just being a boy—and you know what jerks they can be."

"So, what are you going to do about it?" Joey asked.

"Don't you think you should tell Mom and Dad?" Susie suggested. She had come into his room and closed the door. Their mom was downstairs, but she was in her office and wouldn't have been able to hear them anyway. Their dad was still out too. He wouldn't be home until later.

"No."

"Why not?"

Joey was exasperated but he couldn't be mean to Susie, even when she was being a pain in his ass. "Because it is not that big a deal."

"I think it is."

"Well it isn't. I just got pissed off; that's all."

"But you got suspended?"

"It's no big deal. I just got into it with Ms. Priestly and she reported me to the principal. Now I get to stay at home until I am ready to apologize."

"For what?"

"Calling Ms. Priestly a man-hater. She was going on and on about how all the problems in the world were caused by white men. I just couldn't take it anymore."

Even thinking about it got him angry again. These days it just seemed like everybody was dumping on guys like him.

"I'm sure she didn't mean that you were to blame," Susie offered.

"She was going on and on about slavery and all that stuff, and how white men owed everybody else an apology."

"And what did you say?"

"I told her that white men didn't invent slavery and then she started telling everybody that I was an example of white male privilege. In front of all the others."

"Well, I still think you should tell Mom. She would take your side."

"I don't need anybody taking my side. I can fight my own battles."

"Even if it means that you get kicked out of school."

"So what? I am sick of school. All they ever do is pour all their negative crap on us and then tell us that we have to have a good education so that we can have good jobs in a world that is about to come to an end, anyway. It's all bullshit."

"But you have to stay in school."

"Why?"

"So you can go to university."

"Why?"

"So you can get a degree."

"In what? Hating myself? Because that is all they are trying to teach us these days."

"It's not like that, Joey."

"It is for boys. With girls, it's all 'you can be anything you want to be,' but for boys it's all about being told that we have to take the blame for all the stuff that happened in history. I just don't need all that negative crap in my life, anymore."

"So, what are you going to do?"

"I am going to quit school and go work with Dad. At least that way I would be learning how to do things that would be really useful."

"Well then, why don't you tell Mom and Dad that?"

"I will, when the time is right."

Susie stood by the door, looking even more concerned. It got to Joey and he had to go over to her.

"Don't you worry about me, Sis." He took her in his arms and gave her an awkward bear hug. "I'm a big boy now and I can take care of this."

He wanted to pretend to squeeze her like he did when they were little, but she had melted into his arms and was clinging on to him.

Chapter 9

C.C. could not stop thinking about Susie; the poor kid was having a terrible time with everything that was going on. In a way, it reminded C.C. of what she had gone through when she was that age. Back then, she would have given anything to have somebody like the adult version of herself to talk with.

And then there was Joey. He really was a good kid. He was just going through that stage young men had to go through—the one that stretched from fifteen to fifty and some, like the old school guys she had worked with, never outgrew it. Regardless, Joey didn't deserve to be treated that way and just thinking about it made C.C.'s blood boil. She was so sick and tired of people demanding tolerance and acceptance for what they approved of while being totally incapable of extending the same to what they didn't. She had a good mind to go to the school and . . . but it was complicated.

And she shouldn't just go barging in on top of whatever Johnnie and Carol were going through.

For now, she would continue to do what she had been doing. She would continue taking Susie shopping every Saturday. They could invite Joey, too, but she doubted if he would be interested. Still, it was fun and it would keep the doors open. The fact that Susie had called her the other night—and not Gloria—was proof of that. She was growing in Susie's confidence and when the time was right, the opportunity would present itself. Susie would come to her with a problem that only her favorite aunt could resolve. It would be perfect. It would be the unveiling of a whole new and better version of herself; a C.C. 2.0!

She had been reading an article on Feng Shui and almost every word had made her stop and think. Her office and her apartment were fine, tastefully and functionally sparse, it was her mind that was cluttered. She needed to clear out the trappings of everything she had been before and let some new energy flow through her. And she had to open herself up to love. Real love, this time, and not the self-gratifying need for attachment that she had craved up until now—and she needed to be able to give it before she could really receive it.

In the euphoria that had followed that epiphany, life had looked so simple and so clear. Perhaps it always had been, but she had allowed her view to be cluttered by her ambitions, her insecurities, and her anger. Things she now realized were of little value to her anymore.

However, as her many business successes had taught her, an idea without execution was of little value. She would need to put a plan together and she would need to commit herself to it, wholly and thoroughly. But it would have to be altruistic. She wanted to become one of those who, having made it to the top of the ladder, reached down to help others with their climb.

She wanted to share all of that with Heather, but she didn't. That was the old her: *Hey look at me, I am*

*going to transform myself into whatever it is I think
you might want me to be.*

No! This had to be for real, and it had to be something she didn't tell Heather about. It had to be something selfless, and for someone who really needed it.
It was a matter of due diligence, really. It was what it
would take to keep her spirit of renewal alive.

She tapped her fingers on her desk and searched
and searched, but that part of her mind was unchar-
tered territory. It made sense. Up until now, she had
been a business machine and her thoughts automatically turned to strategies, and synergies, and her head
was full of terms like actionable, and bang-for-the-
buck, and core competency.

She might have gotten frustrated, but that would
have been the old version of herself. Instead, she
would make a game of it. *Right*, she told herself. From
this point on, she would do more with less. She would
empower her new ideation and maximize efficiencies.
It would be paradigm shifting, but it would be so much
more than a magic bullet. It would become her new
normal while still being mission critical. It would have
to be scalable and above all else, results oriented when
the rubber hit the road.

She started to laugh at herself, but then she remembered where she was. It was okay. Nobody was
going to come barging into her office. She had read
the riot act at the morning meeting and everyone had
scurried away afterwards and were now busy pretending to be busy. It wasn't very Zen of her, but she
had to; the numbers were so far off target. She had
already adjusted the year end forecast, and cleared it
with her CEO, but it was better to keep that to herself. Sometimes she just had to light little fires under
people's asses. It was how the game was played.

That, she realized, was a big part of her problem; she was now living between two worlds and she was growing so tired of having to play games. She was also growing so tired of having to do all the shitty, little things that she had to do to make her way in the world. It was different before; she had something to prove. She was going to break through the glass ceiling and . . . blah, blah, blah. It wasn't what Heather had actually said, it was more the look on her face.

C.C. had briefly thought about quitting it all; the job, the over-priced condo, the BMW, all of it. All of the things she had once relied on to define who she was. Or to be more correct, who she thought she had wanted to be. She didn't want any of that anymore and it wasn't just Heather's influence. Since that night on the veranda when she talked with Jake—when he apologized for not loving her anyway—she had begun to see herself differently. He may not have been her biological father but if she kept on going the way she was, she was going to end up just like him. At the end, and despite all of the successes in his business life, he was nothing more than a sad and lonely man who desperately sought forgiveness—and approval—from a child who wasn't even his.

That was her crossroads moment. It had cost so little for her to give him that—after she had swallowed her pride and umbrage—, but it was obvious that it meant everything to him. She liked to think that it might have made it easier for him to do what he had to do in the end.

She really wanted to talk with Johnnie and Buddy about that, but it wasn't the right time. It probably never would be. Suicide was one of those things that left a gaping hole in the fabric of life and most people preferred to pretend that it just wasn't there. The old version of herself would not have been so considerate and would have forced them to confront it and they would have reacted in their usual ways, but at least it would have been out there.

But what is the point in that? she asked herself. They all had to find their own way through it.

Johnnie was doing it his way. He was using all of his skills and craft to build a wall between himself and what happened and that was a bit unusual for him. C.C. could only imagine that he still had all kinds of unresolved issues with Jake. It made sense. He was his actual father, albeit an absentee father.

Just thinking about that made her realize something else. C.C. was a little annoyed with him. She wanted to be in there with him, sharing what he was going through. She had told Heather about that the last time they talked, and Heather had said that she might be trying to live vicariously through him, but she didn't say it in a mean way. She said that it was perfectly understandable that C.C. would want to appropriate Johnnie's feelings given that she had been denied the opportunity to have her own.

C.C. wasn't really sure what to make of that and had mentioned it to Johnnie, but he didn't want to talk about it.

"Sounds like someone is blowing pixie dust in your ears," he had laughed, but in a tired way.

"You don't think she is manipulating me?"

"You being manipulated? That I would pay to watch."

"I am not such a bitch, you know."

"I do, but I think that it is funny watching you when you fall in love."

"Asshole!"

"Love you, too, Sis, but right now, I got to run."

She had decided let it go at that, for now. Clearly, he just wasn't ready to go back to where they had been before . . . before their father showed up to kill himself in the only place the family had ever known real peace.

Buddy was probably avoiding it too, though she would never see it that way. She was on some inner pilgrimage to save her marriage and where Norm had once been the cause of everything that was wrong with her, he had now become a gift from the universe and Buddy wasn't worthy—or at least that's the way it sounded from the bits and pieces C.C. had managed to pick up from talking with Susie and Johnnie.

Then it hit her. If she really wanted to clean up her karma, the person she really needed to reach out to was her own sister.

"C.C.? What a wonderful surprise. You know I had been meaning to call you but between the kids going back to school, and Norm has been so busy, and . . . well you know how it is."

"Not really, but I was calling to ask how would you feel about having lunch with me one of these days?"

Buddy sounded genuinely surprised; C.C. had never asked her to lunch before. "I would love that, but are you sure you can spare the time? I know how things must be for you career gals."

C.C. was tempted to ask how she could know, but that would have been mean. Instead, she suggested a time and place. It was a new place in Yorkville that she had heard good things about. And she knew someone there so getting a reservation would not be a problem. It would be her treat, too. That had to be worth a whole heap of 'brownie points.'

*

They were seated right by the front window and while Buddy felt it was like sitting in a fishbowl, C.C. just laughed and said that was the point of it all—being seen in the right places.

"So?" C.C. asked after the waitress brought them their mimosas. Buddy had declined at first, but C.C. had persuaded her. It was her treat and they were going to go all out. "How are the kids?"

"They are fine, now. It took a while to get them settled into the new school year, but that's to be expected—you know, with everything that was going on. Dwayne adapts easily, but Brad struggles with change. He takes after me in that, I suppose. Dwayne is very bright, you know? He should have been in a 'gifted program,' but his school doesn't do that anymore. They say it might stigmatize those kids that can't make it. I don't agree with that, do you? I mean why should the brighter kids be held back. And it is not like Dwayne doesn't help his brother. If he had been put in a gifted program, I am sure that it would have helped Brad, too. He adores his big brother and always tries to imitate everything he does."

C.C. smiled and pretended to be interested. She could never get used to being around the parents of young children.

"Just the other evening," Buddy continued after a quick pause for breath, "Brad was having problems with his homework. Norm was working late and you know me; I never had much of a head for arithmetic. Well, without even waiting to be asked, Dwayne sat down with him and made a game of it all. He had Brad lay out all of his toys so that they could add them, and subtract them, and divide them. It was wonderful to watch. It was one of those moments when you know that you are raising your children properly."

C.C. just sat and kept smiling as she searched for a mantra to intone silently; one that would keep her from interrupting, and one that would keep the look of boredom from her face. Mothers! All they ever did was talk and talk about their children. She forced herself to remember that it was understandable, but it was so tedious. She sipped from her glass and forced herself to smile again.

"A lot of it is down to Norm, you know." Buddy said and nodded while she checked C.C.'s reaction. "I know I wasn't great at giving him credit before, but we all know that I can be a bit of a fusspot, especially around the children. Norm is much more relaxed—not that he lets them get away with anything, either. He can be very strict when the situation calls for it. He just insists that they always try to do their best, but he also seems to understand when to be hard on them and when it is time to back off and let them be kids. He says that kids learn more when they are having fun. And he is right. Just the other day I was reading an article about 'Early Learning.' Have you read it? You should. It explains how we are formed by the time we are five or six and how the things we learn then determine how we react to everything after that. As I read it, I kept thinking about how we were brought up and it really helped me to understand so much. I could send it to you, if you like. It was on a Facebook page called . . . Parenting for Today, or something like that. I will check and send you the link."

"Do, please," C.C. agreed and sipped from her glass. She had read far too many articles on similar ideas, but it would be nice to have something to share with Buddy. Before, she had always turned to Johnnie. She had never really given Buddy the chance to be her big sister.

"I am sorry," Buddy continued after another brief pause for breath and a quick sip from her mimosa. "I don't mean to go on and on. How are things with you and Heather? Any plans on a wedding, or anything like that? Or kids? I think you two would be perfect parents, and I think children growing up in diversity are just as likely to be as happy and successful as any others. Especially with you as a . . . parent. I mean you are a shining example to every little girl growing up. I am so proud to have you as my sister. I know I didn't say it before, but I am. And I am very proud of you for having the courage to come out and be your real self. In a way, it has been a great source of encouragement for me, too, as I go through my own changes."

"Heather and I are fine, thank you. Taking things slowly, but we are doing well."

"Yes. Taking it slow is the best way. I know you might think that your older sister is too much of an old-fashioned fuddy-duddy to understand, but I think it is the way you need to approach it. I was just saying to Norm that . . ."

"Have you talked with Mom lately?" C.C. hadn't meant to interrupt; it was more of a reflex.

"Of course. She calls every week to ask after the kids."

"But have you actually talked with her?" And even as she asked, C.C. regretted it because it seemed to have let all of the air out of Buddy.

"Not much," she sighed and took another sip from her glass. For a moment she looked like she might cry.

"But," she composed herself and continued on with renewed enthusiasm. "Norm and I think it might be better for everyone to step back for a while. Mind you, we are not sure what to do about Christmas. We spent Thanksgiving with Norm's family, but they are going to Arizona for Christmas. Of course, they invited us, but I don't think I would enjoy a hot Christmas. I prefer the old fashioned, snowy kind."

"Do you see much of Johnnie these days?" C.C. asked after a few moments of silence. Buddy seemed to be at a loss for what to say next.

"I had coffee with him the other day. I was just on my way back from returning a dress to that place in Yorkville that you like so much. Do you know Jerome that works there? He is the nicest young man. He's gay and we went for coffee together. I was a little upset about something and he was so nice to me. He understood so much, and he is still so young."

"Jerome? Sure, he and I go way back," C.C. lied. She had no idea who her sister was talking about. "Did Johnnie give you any idea what they are doing for Christmas?"

"No, but he has so much on his mind these days."

"He does? Like what?"

Buddy avoided looking directly at her and C.C. picked up on that. "Tell me."

"Well, it might be nothing—it was just something I saw."

"What?"

"Well, after Jerome and I had coffee together—and we were there for almost two hours—I was walking up Avenue Road and I saw Carol coming out of Scaramouche."

"Really? Is that place still open?"

"I guess so."

"And?"

"Well . . ." Buddy turned away and mumbled. "I can't be certain, but I thought I saw her coming out with another man."

"She does meet clients all the time."

"In Scaramouche?"

"As good a place as any. Maybe he was some rich dude wanting to renovate his place on The Bridle Path."

"Well, he certainly looked like the type."

"And?"

"Well, it's not really for me to say."

"Say what?"

"Well, when they were saying goodbye, he kissed her."

"On the lips?"

"No! On both cheeks."

"How European. Maybe he wants to renovate his summer place in the Algarve. That would suit Johnnie—working in the sun all day."

"Don't you think it was a bit odd?"

"Which part, Scaramouche, the kissing, or the Algarve?"

"The kissing, silly. It just seemed to be overly familiar for two people who just met."

"Did you tell Johnnie?"

"No. Do you think I should?"

Chapter 10

They ordered a second pitcher of beer and grinned at each other. Things had been a bit stiff when they first got together, but they were beginning to loosen up. Johnnie had called—as per Buddy's instructions—and Norm had been delighted. "Sure, Bro, we're overdue a boys' night out. Where do you want to go?" After some humming and hawing, they agreed on McSorley's because the hockey was on and they could both grab cabs home from there.

"So?" Johnnie asked as he stretched his legs out under the table. The crowd at the bar was too young and boisterous so they had moved to a table in the corner where, over the first pitcher, Norm had told him all about his situation at work. "What are you going to do?"

"You don't have to worry about me," Norm laughed with just a hint of beery conviction. "I have a few irons in the fire, already. I'll find something else and, with a bit of luck, I'll be able to walk from one job to the next. Guys like me still have some value in the world."

"Glad to hear that somebody does." Johnnie shrugged and drained his glass.

Norm looked over as he poured more beer. "What's the matter? Is the lord and master of his own destiny suffering from the blahs? Shit, Bro, it's only the middle of November. What are you going to do when the winter comes?"

Johnnie shrugged again, but forced himself to smile. "Hey, I'm just a working stiff. That's more of a management issue. You got to talk with Carol about stuff like that."

"Yeah, I know what you mean, Bro. By the way what's happening with Joey?"

"Oh, you heard about that?"

"I heard he was having some problems at school. Doesn't sound like Joey. What happened?"

"The boy genius got into an argument with one of his teachers and has been expelled until he apologizes."

"What was the argument about?"

"It doesn't matter; he should have known better."

"I don't know, Johnnie. Joey has always been a good kid. Are you sure he is the problem here? I mean you remember what is was like when we were in school, having all those dried out old grodies droning on and on about how hard they had it, and how easy it was for us."

"It still doesn't matter; the kid should know better."

"So, what's going to happen?"

"As far as I am concerned, he's going to go back and apologize." Johnnie sounded so adamant, like he was trying to convince someone.

"Then what?"

"Then he is going to keep his nose clean and graduate so he has some hope of getting into whatever university might give him a chance at doing something with his life."

"I don't know about all of that, Johnnie." Norm tried to sound conciliatory. He didn't want it to seem like he was disagreeing. "Why can't he work for you? The kid loves working with his hands and not everybody is cut out for sitting behind a desk all day."

Johnnie didn't answer and sipped his fresh beer like he was thinking about it. Norm might have pushed the matter, but the Leafs scored and the crowd at the bar erupted in a frenzy of high-fives, burly chest bumps, and a few derogatory comments towards the skeptics among them.

"You heard it here, first," Norm said loudly as everyone around them began to chant Go-Leafs-go. He tapped in time on the table and looked as convincing as he could. "We're going all the way this year."

"Yeah, right," Johnnie laughed sardonically. "Until they choke in the play-offs."

"C'mon, Johnnie. Don't be like that. You got to believe."

"In what?"

"Hockey, man. It's all guys like us have got left and we should enjoy it while we can. One of these days some of those do-gooders are going to come along and try to ban it."

The Leafs scored again, right from the face-off, and again everyone around them erupted and repeated their rituals, but with even more enthusiasm. It was still very early in the season, but it was Toronto against Montreal—the oldest and most bitter rivalry in hockey.

"You know," Norm said after they had ordered a plate of wings from the young woman who smiled at them like they were harmless old men. "If they can just get the power-play clicking . . . I mean their penalty killing is pretty good, but they've got to start putting teams away when they get the chance." He was beginning to feel warm inside and he wanted things with Johnnie to be the way they used to be. He topped up their glasses and raised his to toast: "All the way this year."

Johnnie clinked his glass and shook his head. "To the stupidity of eternal optimism."

It might have been the beer, or it might have been that he was just enjoying hanging-out with his brother-in-law, but Norm had to ask. "Johnnie?"

"Yeah?"

"Do you want to tell me what's really eating you? Because from where I'm sitting, a guy like you has it made."

Johnnie grimaced like even the idea of talking about himself was painful. "Can we just have a few beers and not talk about all that stuff?"

"We can, if that's what you want. But let me just say one thing. You work for yourself and you get to do what you love doing. In my book, that is having it made. I mean look at me. I just finished busting my guts trying to get something done for my corporate overlords and what do they do when I finish it?" He got a little agitated and slapped his hand on the table. "I mean, would it have killed them to give me something for all of that?"

"They did. They gave you a nice pink slip."

"That's my point, Bro. Would it have made such a dent in their precious balance sheet to treat a guy fairly?" He raised his glass and pointed it at Johnnie. "You have no idea how good you really have it."

Johnnie also raised his glass, but stopped and looked inside. "Tell me something," he asked without looking up. "If you really think working for yourself is so great, why aren't you doing it?"

"Come on, Johnnie. You know; it has never been the right time."

"I can't think of a better time," Johnnie winked at him. "After all, soon you are going to have nothing better to do. Besides, it's never the right time. The kids are always too young, or the markets are doing badly. There's always ninety-nine reasons for not doing it."

"Yeah, maybe you're right," Norm agreed and looked into his glass.

"Yeah, maybe I am," Johnnie nodded and took another drink. "But then, what the hell do I know about anything?"

"See! Right there," Norm leaned forward for emphasis. "That's what I'm talking about. You do know. You know what is real because you are doing it." Norm sat back like he had scored a point, but Johnnie just shook his head.

"You know, we are in the same boat, when you think about it? You are about to lose your job and I have only one lined up for next year—maybe two, if we get really lucky."

He drained his glass again and Norm reached for the pitcher. "Here's an idea," he laughed as he began to pour. "Maybe you and I should go into business together."

"Doing what?"

"That's just details," Norm laughed after he had refilled both glasses. "We can figure all that out later."

"I am beginning to see why they fired you."

"Maybe," Norm agreed after taking a drink. "But at the very least we should get ourselves one of those mission statements. It's not like it really has to mean anything, but everybody else has one. You know, the sort of thing that all the fancy companies put on shiny plaques: 'Our primary focus is to always provide maximum value for our shareholders while screwing over our customers and employees, alike.'"

"Hey, I like that. It's refreshingly honest."

They were still smirking at that when the young woman brought the wings. Half were hot and the other half were honey-garlic. They both reached for them like they hadn't eaten in days.

"Let's drink to it then."

They wiped their fingers and clinked glasses before draining them. The beer was really kicking in and they were starting to drift past all the cares and worries they had brought in with them. The Leafs scored again and that just made everything perfect—or as perfect as life could be on a cold November night in the Great, White North.

"But we are going to need a name." Norm suddenly grew more serious as the pile of chicken bones grew. "Something that reflects who we are and what we are really about."

"I got it," Johnnie burped a little. It had been some time since they had spent a night drinking and it was catching up on them. Not to mention the hot wings, they should have gone with mild. "It has to be something with the word 'Dinosaurs' in it."

"I don't get it."

"You will when you have been out of work for a while. Face it, Norm. Guys like us are becoming extinct."

"Yeah," Norm muttered and stared into his glass. Then he looked up like a thought had just occurred to him. "Can I ask you something?"

"The first rule of the ancient order of the Dinosaur Club is no thinking or asking about stuff."

"That sounds more like two rules."

"Okay then, no talking about stuff you have to think about."

"Okay, but you know me. I'm not great at thinking, I just say whatever comes into my mind."

"Okay then, but just one question."

"What happened between you and your old man and what is going on between you and Carol?"

"That's none of your business and nothing happened. My old man died. Shit happens."

"And Carol?"

"She doesn't like when shit happens."

Norm decided to let it go at that and gestured towards the bar for one more pitcher. Buddy had told him about Carol and the guy outside the restaurant. And she had said that he should try to find a way of mentioning it to Johnnie, but he couldn't. It wasn't the way things were done. Besides, he was in no position to be poking around in other people's marriages. Things with Buddy were okay again—even though he had messed up on date night—but every day he didn't tell her about the situation at work, he felt like he was cheating on her. The young woman brought the beer and cleared away the chicken bones and the pile of sticky napkins. She also left a few wet wipes and gave both of them her sweetest smile.

"I have decided," Norm explained as he refilled their glasses. "That if I am going to be an unemployed bum, I need to develop a drinking problem too."

"How you going to pay for it, genius? Don't expect me to give you handouts."

"I don't. I have decided that I am going to win a million dollars and spend it all on beer."

"Buying lotto tickets again?"

"Nay, that's just for losers and I'm not there yet. Maybe in a few months, but not yet."

"That should be our motto: We're not desperate, yet."

"We could get t-shirts, and hats."

"Can't; it's not in the budget."

"I'll pay for them—out of my million."

They both laughed at that, but it was a hollow laugh. A type of laugh that comes from those who had spent so much of their time putting on braver faces. Those who were usually so careful not to let their kids, or their partners, see the side of them that struggled to keep going. But here, in each other's company, relaxed and more carefree as the beer coursed through them, they could let their guards down. They knew each other well enough by now; well enough to trust each other with whatever floated up from deep inside of them.

"Buddy was telling me that she had coffee with you the other day," Norm mentioned casually to break the silence. "And she says that she is a bit worried about you."

*

Johnnie knew it would come up. Buddy would have worked on Norm, too. He just wasn't sure what to say about all of that. He might have said that his sister was always worried about something, but he didn't. Buddy was trying so hard and he didn't want to say or do anything that might mess that up for her.

Or he might have told Norm what Buddy was really worried about, but he didn't do that, either. It wasn't his to tell. Instead, he just shrugged. "Yeah? I guess she just caught me on a bad day."

"She is worried that you haven't been the same since your father died." Norm ventured again. He sounded tentative, but Johnnie understood. Usually, these types of conversations happened the other way around.

Norm was worried, too. Buddy had told him that she sensed things weren't right with her brother and that Norm should try to find out what was really bothering him. He didn't have to be asked a second time. He wanted to be there for Johnnie the way Johnnie had been there for him so many times before. "She thought you might want to talk about things."

Johnnie said nothing and Norm wasn't sure what to do. If it was the other way around Johnnie would have got him talking. He always knew how to draw Norm out of himself. He had done it so often.

"You know," Norm continued, "you can talk to me about anything."

"Like what?"

"Like stuff you might not be comfortable talking with others about. We are like brothers, you and me, and we have been through a lot of shit together."

Johnnie looked him up and down like he was deciding something and then slowly nodded his head. "You're right, Norm. And here's something I can only share with you. I am going to go and take a leak."

He was still laughing about that as he made his way through the crowd at the bar, clutching their glasses and staring up at the TV screens. They made way for him because he was big and he was lurching a bit, though a few of them shared jokes with him as he passed. Norm stared at his beer and didn't feel so good about himself. When Buddy had told him about Carol and the guy, she said something that had gotten stuck inside of him. "It is probably nothing," she had said. "But I think Johnnie should know about it. You would want to know if it was you, wouldn't you?" But by the time Johnnie got back, he had decided to let it drop. Boys' night out wasn't the place for that type of thing. It was more about letting off some steam. Instead, he got up to relieve himself and it took him a lot longer to make his way through the crowd.

*

Johnnie watched him with mixed feelings. Norm was the type of guy who let himself get pushed around far too easily. And yet here they were, together, sharing a few pitchers and staring into a bleak future. Johnnie would figure it out, but Norm . . . Norm was going to need all the help he could get.

It took him forever to make his way back to the table. The Leafs scored again and he was trapped in the celebration that ensued. Watching him, Johnnie decided: he would let him in. Norm just wanted to feel a part of anything that Johnnie was going through and there was no one else he felt comfortable talking with about it. Except Gloria.

"You know when you asked me about what was eating me?" he announced when Norm had gotten back to his seat. "Well here it is. That weekend at the cottage, my old man asked me to help him kill himself. Just don't go blabbing about it to everyone."

"Shit Johnnie. I had no idea. I mean . . . what the fuck?"

"What the fuck, is right. I couldn't do it and that has me all messed-up inside."

Norm had nothing to say to that. What could he possibly say? Instead they sat drinking their beer and watching the crowd around them. Everyone else was happy. The Leafs won five to one and the smart asses among them were already talking about planning the parade.

Chapter 11

C.C. did not have to wait very long for her chance to roll out the new and improved C.C. 2.0. Susie's high school had contacted C.C.'s company to ask if they could recommend a speaker for their Futures Program; *a student led initiative to help prepare aspiring careerists for the lives that lay ahead of them.* In a politely worded email, reviewed and approved by Ms. Priestly and the principal, they had stated their preference for a strong, successful career woman who would be willing to visit the school and share her opinions and experiences with a gathering of interested students.

This was it. This was her chance to strut her stuff in front of Susie and all her friends, but C.C. still managed to act surprised when her CEO called her into his office and broached her about doing it. He said it would provide the perfect opportunity to showcase what a forward-thinking, and progressive organization they were.

"We take immense pride and satisfaction in our stated policy that we will never allow color, gender, or sexual orientation to be used as a barrier against merited advancement," he said in that polished voice he used when he was presenting to the Board. "And I cannot think of anyone more suited to represent us in that than you?"

C.C. had allowed herself to smile when she got back to her office. He wasn't the worst boss she'd ever had even if, behind his humane facade, he really didn't care who anybody was as long as they were making the numbers. But, while he could be ruthless with those who didn't, he was also the one who had signed off on C.C.'s various promotions for one simple reason; she had always delivered.

The school principal had been cautious when she called to confirm and C.C. could only imagine that the matter of Joey was lurking in the back of his mind, but she had made no reference to it. Instead, she had told him that she would be delighted to participate and would offer whatever insights she had that might be of any help in preparing the next generation for the world that awaited them.

She had also made a point of registering that she was openly gay and hoped that would not be an issue. He had gushed to assure her that it wouldn't be and that the school's stated policy was to embrace diversity and it strongly encouraged its students to be open-minded and tolerant. C.C. had also smiled at that and began to plan her presentation.

After she had introduced herself, and had placed special emphasis on her title, C.C. paused and looked around the auditorium. Half of the kids looked bored and more than a few looked skeptical. She hesitated for a moment and looked down at her notes. She'd had Susie take a look at them in case they sounded condescending. She didn't want that. She didn't want to be another talking suit that showed up to sell a load of corporatism. She wanted the kids in the audience to be able to see a part of themselves in her. She just couldn't decide on which part that should be.

To establish credulity, she proudly rhymed off her long list of achievements then put her notes down and stepped out from behind the podium. She wanted to engage with her audience directly. She had worn her mid-length black skirt and pin striped jacket over a dark red shirt that matched her lipstick. And she was wearing her dark red high heels. She was not a pants suit type of girl: that would have been too much of a cliché.

"And now that I have boasted about how wonderful I am," she joked. "I want to tell you a little bit about what I believe to be really important for life in general—and particularly for a life in business." She paused and looked down to where Ms. Priestly was sitting in the front row, right in front of Susie and her friends.

"You see, back when I was in high school, I was the most awkward and insecure kid. Some of you would have felt sorry for me, and most of you would probably have been mean to me." That made some of the kids sit up.

"Yeah. That's right. When I started high-school—back at the end of the last millennium—no one had any time for such things as tolerance or diversity. Back then you had to fit in with one clique or another and because I was what is called a 'late bloomer'— I had buck teeth and no breasts—, I was never accepted by the popular kids.

"Please understand," she said after the few nervous laughs had died away. "I am not telling you this to try to get you to feel sorry for me. I am telling you this because even though I hated every single day, and never really fitted in, I went along with it because that is what we have to do in high schools. We have to go along with whatever is happening because we are too afraid to stand out and really be ourselves." She paused again to scan the room. More of the kids were paying attention now, and the principal and Ms. Priestly were nodding their heads.

"Now while that might seem like a good coping strategy when you are young and unsure of yourself, if you are planning on becoming anything in life, please stop it. Please stop trying to be what others think you should be." She paused again for effect. They were a difficult crowd to read.

"I say that because I am sure that many of you are already wondering how you are going to fit in with the adult world—and particularly the business world." She paused again and paced back and forth like she was deep in thought; it was what people did in TED Talks. Then she looked out at her audience and asked: "How should you prepare for fitting into the business world?"

No one responded, but she didn't expect them to.

"Well, I am sure you have all heard about the things business says it's looking for: Team-players who are not afraid to think outside of the box; goal-oriented individuals who are willing to go the extra mile, smart people, savvy people, and all of those wonderful things."

She looked out at all the young faces. Some nodded along like she had confirmed what they had learned to believe while others still looked a little bored. "But what does any of that really mean?"

Heather had recently asked her the same question and C.C. had been forced to stop and think about it.

"What is a team player?" she asked and let her question float around the room.

"Is it someone who goes along with things because everybody else does?

"Is it somebody who does not rock the boat even when it is heading for the rocks?

"If you want my opinion, I think the business world has far too many of those already. They may seem to be ideally suited, but it has been my experience that they can quickly become the dead weight that drags everybody else down. For me, a team player is someone who will work with others, but is not afraid to stand up and lead in a better direction."

It was what she had done, many times. And while she had advanced because of it, she had also pissed off a lot of former colleagues. At the time, she hadn't given it a second thought. But lately . . .

"As for thinking outside the box? I am not so sure that is something corporate culture really looks kindly on. Yes, if you are a true innovator and can come up with something that is unique and brilliant, and you have the means to demonstrate that it is viable, someone will come along and give you a big bag of money for it. You know what I mean: things like the next 'killer app.'"

That got a few more heads nodding, particularly among the techy crowd.

"Now, while that might work for the one in a hundred, I have to be honest and tell you that it has become more of a catch phrase that few in business really understand anymore.

"It has been my experience that, internally, corporate culture tends to be more conservative and cautious and usually rewards those who support that, rather than those who would speak against it. So, if you are planning to think outside the box, be prepared to spend a lot of time outside of that box—on your own.

"And then we come to goal-oriented and this is where I have some real issues."

She and Heather had discussed it. How could you promote a common cause in an environment that celebrated individual effort?

"Far too many businesses rely on individual bonuses to reward their employees and sometimes that can have a very negative impact, but what is the alternative?"

She hadn't been able to find one, human nature being what it was. Heather had argued that it wasn't human nature—that is was more the result of corporate conditioning.

"I am sure that you all have experience working on group projects. And I am sure you are all familiar with the types of problems working like that can create. Every group will have those who do not pull their own weight, as well as those who are quick to try to take credit for what others have done."

That got even more heads nodding.

"That, in my opinion, is probably the biggest challenge that business management faces. Do you reward the individual who runs roughshod over everyone else to get to the finishing line, or do you reward the group for pulling together?

"Also, do you reward practices that deliver immediate results, but might have long-term negative impact? These are the questions that keep corporate executives up at night—or they should."

C.C. paused to smile to herself. These were the very same questions that she had disregarded for years. Instead, she had kept her nose clean and did whatever she had to do to make the numbers, rarely stopping to consider the costs. But that was before she met Heather.

"In many ways schools and business are very similar. Both are preoccupied with numbers. For business it is all about sales figures and for schools, it is all about grades and test performance. Now, while both can seem valid enough, the question that the truly smart and savvy must really ask is: is that not a bit too short term?" Even as she asked that question, she knew. She had arrived at that point in her life where she could no longer go on doing what she had done without question.

"Over the last few decades, more and more schools have become fixated on preparing students for a life in business. Many of you will graduate and go on to take some type of business degree. Some of you might even end up with MBAs." C.C. paused for a moment. She was about to say something she had never said before. "If you want my opinion, don't. Stop wasting your time, and your parents' money, learning the jargon and the rituals of business. Instead, go out and learn something about the world we actually live in.

"I realize that many of you will think that is an odd thing for a corporate, like me, to say, but it is not just me. Just look at the recent hiring trends of major tech companies. They are hiring Liberal Arts graduates. Why?

"Is it because the mass production of supposed specialists who know so little of the world outside of business is quickly revealing itself to be its own evolutionary dead-end?"

The principal was uneasy in his seat, but most of the kids were paying attention, now.

"Or is it because business, as we know it, is rushing to its own logical conclusion?

"With increased profit and constant growth as the only values we measure business and economic heath by, we overlook the cold, hard fact that we are consuming and discarding at a rate that is not sustainable for the planet, or for business itself. And this is not just in the cases of material or physical resources. We are also consuming and discarding the most valuable assets we have; our people.

"Over the last few years, I have had the opportunity to work with recent graduates from some of the better business schools around the country and with very few exceptions, most of them get a nasty shock when they are thrown into the deep end. It is all very well learning the approved answers and being able to recite case studies but unless you can think on your feet, you might find that your degree is nothing more than a ticket to some sideshow.

"What this approach has not yet realized is the unchanging fact that even the most dynamic and innovative businesses depend on the type of skills that are not being taught anymore. I am referring to the old-fashioned type of skills that people learned working their way up from the mailroom.

"We continue to confuse education with intelligence and disregard the natural skills and instincts that are probably far more important. Not to mention the most important ingredient for success. Real passion.

"Please don't misunderstand me. I am not telling you this to discourage you but unless business is your real passion, go into something else. I have seen too many starry-eyed kids burn out and become sad and tragic people. People who had subscribed to an idea that had been sold to them by their parents, or their teachers, and were now confronted with the reality of their choices. Too many of them were there because they thought that was what they wanted, or because it was expected of them.

"Think about that. Then think about what people like that will become. Think about what happens to people who give up their lives to do things they later realize they had never really wanted to do." That was what she had done. She had spent far too many years seeking validation and now that she had it, it wasn't enough.

"It has often been said that the key to real and satisfying success is to find what you love doing. Once who have that part figured out, all you have to do is to find a way of doing it." And even as she stood there in front of a hundred high school kids, C.C. made a pact with herself. From now on, she would strive to live by those words, anything else would be hypocritical. But how?

"Of course, finding what you love can take time. And it might mean trying all sorts of jobs or careers for no other reason than to rule out the things you don't want to do.

"Why am I telling you this?

"Because it should be more than obvious to any-body who stops and thinks about it that the way we conduct ourselves has to change. Most of your generation are already keenly aware of the environmental and social costs of the outdated practices and models we cling to. You know that has to change."

The principal and Ms. Priestly did not seem too impressed, but most of the kids were now sitting up and taking in everything she said. She felt good about that. Someone had to tell them the truth.

"And if the young men here don't mind, I would like to address the young women I see sitting out there. You have been brought up in a culture that seeks to rectify bias and discrimination against you. You have been encouraged to think that anything is possible for you and that there are no barriers that you cannot break through. I agree with all of that, but only up to a point.

"There are still relics of the old days around; men who will think, and say, that you should be home raising children and stupid things like that. Thankfully, they are a dying breed. However, you will be faced with a far more discerning evaluation. Regardless of your color, gender or sexual orientation you will be evaluated on what you actually bring to the show.

"Sure, there are organizations that will hire to fill quotas and such things—usually government or public sector jobs—and they have a place in the grand scheme of things. But if you really want to test yourself in the big leagues, forget all of that. It won't matter. What will matter is what is inside of you. Do you have what it takes? And sadly, it has been my experience that very few women do." That ruffled a few feathers so C.C. paused and took a drink for from the water glass that had been left for her.

"I will say it again: in my experience, very few women have what it takes.

"Now I realize that a comment like that can leave me open to accusations of misogyny—and yes women are just as likely to be guilty of that as men. I say it because, for most women, there comes a point where hard choices have to be made. Do you have a career, or do you have a family?" And that was it. That was one of the burning questions she had to ask herself and Heather.

"Now for years we have had a great many well-intentioned people trying to convince us that today's women can have both—that women can have it all. Perhaps that is true in some case but from what I have seen, hard compromises have to be made. The lucky women are those who have partners that can pick up the slack at home. For others, it is a constant conflict that usually means that somebody is short-changed; their employer, their children, or their partners.

"I have seen it so many times. Young women who are bright and full of potential until their biological clocks go off. Then they are subjected to pressures that are so distracting and many of them start to fall behind. I don't mean to be the bearer of bad news, but corporate culture cares little for your home/work balance.

"So, what is my reason for saying all of this?

"It is this. Choose a career in business because you want to and not because it is expected of you. Choose it because you thrive in a no-holds-barred environment, because that is what you will be stepping into—unless, of course, you have the type of connections that can propel you far higher than you own efforts ever could," she added with just a hint of a smirk. She had encountered a few of them. Privileged sons of the old boy network and she had eaten them alive.

"Also, you should do it to challenge yourself for your own sake and not because you want to be trail-blazers for whatever subset of the human race you have chosen to identify with.

"And be prepared to be challenged by others. Be prepared for rivals to come at you with everything they have. Be prepared to have every little weakness and flaw detected and used against you because that is the way the world is.

"Forget all this equality stuff, it won't apply. Forget about getting offended by what people might say or do, that is a weakness. Forget about the idea that the world owes you something.

"And, again for you young women here today, always remember this: your female colleagues will often be your worst friends. The sisterhood, Feminism, solidarity, all of that stuff will go flying out the window when there is a promotion at stake. And when you win it, expect to hear the rumors that you slept your way to the top—even if you are like me; gay." That induced a number of nervous giggles and confused looks from the principal and Ms. Priestly, but C.C. didn't care. She was on a mission.

"So, my advice to you is this. If you are going to choose this life, forget about barriers and glass ceilings and all the other buzzwords that you may have heard. Men, and women, are not your enemies, they are your competition and whining about them will only damage your own credibility.

"So, I will leave you now with the wise words of Sun Tzu who wrote: 'It is said that if you know your enemies and know yourself, you will not be imperiled in a hundred battles; if you do not know your enemies but do know yourself, you will win one and lose one; if you do not know your enemies nor yourself, you will be imperiled in every single battle.'"

Chapter 12

After C.C. had finished talking to the kids at Susie's high school, and the principal had publicly thanked her, he asked her to join him, Ms. Priestly, and the student council, in his office. The Futures Program had a very active Facebook page and they wanted a few photos for their posts about the event.

C.C. agreed but as soon as the kids had left, she casually raised the matter of Joey's suspension. She wondered if it might not be a good time to try to find some resolution. She felt like she was on a roll and decided to try to kill two birds with one stone.

The principal nodded and said he had expected the matter to come up. He exchanged a quick glance with Ms. Priestly and began by telling C.C. that he had been the principal for almost three years, and had been teaching for more than fifteen before that. He also mentioned that, during that time, he had personally dealt with hundreds of students and that the situation with Joey was not unique. It was, in his opinion, a problem that could easily be rectified.

He did, however, stress that it was of vital importance that young men, like Joey, were made aware that certain types of behavior were no longer acceptable. "As educators," he said with a quick glance in

Ms. Priestley's direction. "We feel it is our responsibility to force these young men to address their issues before they became stigmatized by them and carry that through the rest of their lives."

"That does sound fair," C.C. acknowledged. "And may I ask what, exactly, is the problem with Joey?"

C.C. then listened politely as Ms. Priestly explained that she had concerns regarding Joey and that she sensed that he might be developing misogynistic tendencies. She was also concerned that when she tried to raise those issues with him, that he was arrogant and disrespectful, and showed many of the signs of toxic masculinity.

The principal nodded along and added that the school was particularly concerned about that type of thing and that theirs was an environment of inclusion and acceptance.

Ms. Priestly then went on to explain that they were particularly curious as to why Joey's parents had not been in contact. She had hoped that they would have engaged with her to help Joey overcome his issues.

"Up until recently, Joey has been a wonderful student. He has been very bright and inquisitive, but lately we are seeing a surlier, uncooperative side of him. All of this makes me wonder if there might be problems in the home? That is usually where these types of issues begin."

"We see so much of that from our perspective," the principal agreed. "Particularly with boys who are at that critical age."

They were both cautious and a little nervous, so C.C. waited until they were finished.

She also needed a few moments to try to regain control of her emotions. Whatever reason Johnnie and Carol had for not contacting the school would have been a valid one and no one outside the family could second-guess that. No one.

"I understand," Ms. Priestly added. "That Joey's grandfather recently passed away and I was wondering if that might be the root of the issue. After all, how families cope with such things can be a major influence on children."

C.C. was losing her inner battle.

"And that," Ms. Priestly concluded. "Is why we were hoping that Joey's parents would engage with us, so that we could offer our support and guidance."

Carol had often said that they were like the Corleone family and she had a point. Growing up with all the hysterics and the drama, they had built a wall around themselves. Carol also suggested that they were like a cult, but usually she was joking. Still, any criticism of her family caused C.C.'s hackles to rise so she took a deep breath.

"May I ask how old are you?" she turned and smiled at Ms. Priestly.

"Twenty-eight."

"And do you have children?"

"Not yet, but someday," the young teacher answered with a blush.

"Are you gay or straight?"

Before Ms. Priestly could answer, the principal interrupted to say that such a question could be considered inappropriate.

C.C. just smiled at that. "My reason for raising it," she explained, "is because when I came out, my entire family was, and remains, nothing but supportive." It wasn't totally true, but her mother and Buddy were slowly coming around. "And I mention that because in my family, judgmental views are discouraged."

The principal nodded at that. "And that is also something we strongly approve of."

"That is nice that you should say that, but neither I, nor my family, need anybody's approval. As I have just finished explaining to your students, I began as a Sales Rep and am now a V.P. at a very large and successful corporation. I have coped with all the challenges such a career trajectory can entail even though I was openly gay." It wasn't entirely true, but C.C. was trying to make a point. "I am, if you like, the very person that you hope your students might aspire to become."

Both the principal, and Ms. Priestly nodded along, cautiously.

"However, I wonder if either of you could fully appreciate how I achieved what I did. In short, it was because I was willing to stand up for myself and not rely on current consensus and the approval of others—another thing that is strongly encouraged in my family.

"And it has been my experience that those who develop dependencies on such things are doomed to mediocrity and end up in menial jobs."

They both stiffened at that.

"Also, I would like to remind both of you that a significant part of my professional responsibility is to mentor some of the young people who work for us." She paused long enough to look both of them in the eye. She was feeling angry, and she was feeling vindictive. She briefly thought about her new resolve, but to hell with that. This was about her family.

"And while it is something that I particularly enjoy, I am sorry to say that I have found that the biggest challenge is how unprepared they are for the reality of their chosen field. I have given it considerable thought and I believe the problem stems from the way they are educated."

They both sat up a little straighter, but were now reluctant to look at her.

"I have also given considerable thought to what might be done about that and I have come to believe that it is primarily a matter of managing expectations." She felt like she was dressing down her sales managers and that made her feel so good.

"Now," she added a reflective tone to her voice. "While I am sure we are all in favor of encouraging these young people, and helping them to build the self-confidence they will need, I have also come to believe that we might be doing them a huge disservice."

She paused again, for effect and to make eye contact.

"Currently, we are presenting them with a view of the world that might be little more than some fantastical utopia that, in the reality of our times, is nothing more than wishful thinking and the projection of unfounded theories. That said, my recommendation to all concerned with their well-being is that we consider going back to teaching them how to deal with the world the way it really is."

"I can assure you," Ms. Priestly interrupted with a haughty tone. "That as a feminist and an educator, I am very aware of what role we must play in shaping our future."

"May I ask," C.C. smiled. "What other work experience you have?"

"I have been a teacher since I graduated."

"I see. And did you work while you were a student?"

"Well . . . not really, but I did volunteer at summer camps. I was very fortunate to have well-established parents, but I am very conscious of my privilege and believe strongly in giving back to society."

"That is very gracious of you, but do you really believe that any of this makes you qualified to offer your students a perspective of proven value?"

The principal tried to interject, but C.C. cut him off. "As someone who spends her days out in the real world, and as someone who has broken through the glass ceiling, and as someone who has done all of that as an openly gay woman, I would think that I might be far more qualified to evaluate the results of such efforts. And I am sorry to tell you that they are often found to be sub-par."

Ms. Priestly stammered a bit. "Please know," she almost pleaded, "that I have nothing but the greatest admiration for strong, brave, independent women like you. In fact, this is the very thing we are trying to teach our young women. To be brave and to stand up to men."

"Men?" C.C. almost snorted. "Men may not be the biggest problem these young women face. I have found that the reason most women shy away from the challenge of a career is that they fear the opinions of other women.

"Yes, I said it, and any woman who chooses a career over family will confirm this. Any woman who has really succeeded will tell you this.

"And, as a woman who has done both, I can also tell you that it has been my experience that men did not gossip behind my back. It wasn't men who whispered that I must have slept my way to the top." Some had, until they found out she was gay.

"With all due respect," the principal tried again, but C.C. was having none of it. She had built up a head of steam and was now venting her indignation in all her self-righteous glory—something Johnnie and Carol had often teased her about. And she was enjoying every moment of it.

"I don't need your respect and I don't want it."

She really didn't. He reminded her of all those castrated men who clung to their little positions of power by agreeing to everything and in the end stood for nothing. Middle management was full of them.

"And you," she pointed at Ms. Priestly. "You preach tolerance but the first time you are faced with someone who challenges you, you try to publicly shame them."

"I did no such thing," Ms. Priestly interrupted.

"Really? And what were your comments about 'white male privilege' meant to convey? People like you make life so much more difficult for the real women in the world. You sit here in your little politically correct enclaves and preach your unproven theories to kids who have no choice but to put up with your nonsense. If you really want to make a difference in the real world, then go out and do something in it."

"Well," the principal finally managed to interject. "Thank you for explaining your views so clearly, but I think we are done here." He rose and stepped towards the door, but C.C. remained seated.

"There is one more thing that I would share with you before I leave. In business, we value the art of making the deal and this is what I am going to ask of both of you. You will reinstate my nephew immediately and withdraw any suggestion that he was at fault."

"I am afraid that will not be possible."

"Very well, then. You leave me with no other option than to have the matter dealt with elsewhere."

"Meaning?" the principal asked and it was obvious that he was nervous.

"Meaning that I have a great many friends in the media and this little episode is the type of thing many of them would be more than happy to give coverage to. Can you just imagine how it would play out: Openly gay, successful career woman campaigns for freedom of speech against two insipid little social engineers? I doubt that would be the type of coverage your school board would like to see. And now, I will leave you to get on with your busy little days."

She rose and walked out, feeling really good about herself.

And that, she smiled to herself as she climbed into her shiny little Barbie car, *is how a strong, independent woman deals with nonsense.*

Over the next few days, C.C. began to feel a little conflicted about her trip to the school. A part of her felt like an avenger, but another part of her felt like a bully—a feeling she had never experienced before. For most of her life she had always seen herself as the victim, and that had worked so well for her. It had allowed her to deflect responsibility for her own actions and it had driven her to strive harder than anyone around her. But now, and no matter how much she tried to rationalize it, what she had done to Ms. Priestly just felt a little spiteful, and malicious. She briefly considered talking with Heather about it, but she knew what she would say.

Besides, she didn't want to run to Heather with every little thing that was happening in her life. Instead, she reviewed the whole episode and couldn't help but cringe a little. It had been way too much, but she could learn from that. From now on she would have to conduct her personal life as she did her business life; professionally, carefully, and constructively.

She was still thinking about all of that when her phone rang. It was Carol.

"Well hello there, stranger," C.C. answered as she rearranged her thoughts. Carol always had a way of making her feel so juvenile.

"Yeah, hi. Listen the reason I am calling is to tell you that I just got a call from the school. It would seem that your presentation had quite an impact."

"Oh?" C.C. wanted to sound surprised but inside, she had been hoping that Carol would call.

"Yes. They called to tell me that Joey's suspension has been lifted and he can return to school."

"And you called to thank me? There's no need."

Just the idea that Carol might approve of what she had done was enough to dispel her previous misgivings and without thinking C.C. added: "I really enjoyed putting those smug prigs in their place. Besides, I would do anything for your kids, you know that."

"Yes, I know that, but I do wish you had checked with me before you went and did whatever it was that you did."

"What do you mean?"

"Well, for one thing, Joey is not very happy with you right now."

"Really? I suppose he feels that having his aunt fight his battles is . . ."

"That's not the problem."

"No?"

"No. Joey wanted to quit school and go work with his father. But his father—your wonderful big brother—would not even consider it."

"Oh!"

"Yes, oh! I was working on Johnnie and I think he was just about to come around. But now . . ."

"Oh, shit!"

"Precisely."

"Oh, Carol. I am so sorry. Is there anything I can do? Maybe if I talked with Johnnie?"

"I wouldn't, if I were you. He's also pretty pissed at you right now."

"Me? What does he have to be pissed about? If anything, he should be happy. He got what he wanted."

"That's not the way he sees it. As far as he is concerned, the issue was between Joey and the school and he would have preferred if you had left it that way."

"I am so sorry, Carol. But I am sure I can smooth things over with Johnnie."

"Don't take this the wrong way, C.C., but smoothing things over has never been your strongest suit. And, if you want my opinion, I would suggest that you stay out of it for a while and let things settle on their own."

C.C. wasn't sure if it was a reprimand, or a rebuke. Carol could always make her feel like that.

"I don't suppose," she ventured cautiously, "that you would consider lunch one of these days? It would be my treat—to make up for what I did."

"Sure, but let me get back to you on that." Carol responded automatically and C.C. did not detect much enthusiasm in her voice. It sounded more like Carol was accepting it as an obligation.

The cheeky side of her wanted to suggest that they go to Scaramouche, but she didn't.

She did, however, consider telling Carol that Buddy had seen her there. And that she had probably told Johnnie.

C.C. stopped and gave it some thought and decided that it wasn't her just being petty and vindictive. Whatever was going on, it would better out in the open because Johnnie had a right to know.

And, she was sure that Carol would have a perfectly reasonable explanation.

Chapter 13

By the dying days of November, when the nights were longer and colder, Gloria's nightmares had become darker and darker. Every night, by the light of a Mourning Moon, she followed her own footprints out to the island. The air was always still, but sometimes she could hear a coyote yipping from the shadows of the trees. It never concerned her and she just kept on walking while her heartbeat throbbed in her ears and her snow shoes crunched through the brittle rime.

Every time she got there, she would fall to her knees and call out Jake's name, over and over; her voice resonating with all of the anguish that was inside of her and echoing across the frozen lake to the trees on the far side. Sometimes the coyote would stop to listen, and other times it joined in.

Time after time she dropped to her knees and began to scratch at the frozen surface of the lake, even as her nails began to break and her fingers began to bleed. But she could never stop.

Then, as her only son's bloated face began to fade and drift away into the depths, she would finally manage to make a small crack in the ice. She always cried out again, pleading with him to come back to her. Pleading as she pounded frantically on the ice with her bare fists as her old, frail knuckles quickly became bruised and bloodied, but she could never stop. She had to try to make the slender crack large enough to fit her arm through.

When it finally was, she always called his name again and plunged her arm down into the cold, dark lake. She could not see anything in the murky water so she had to grope around, even as her arm grew colder and whiter. She never cared about any of that, she just could not give up. And, just as she was about to lose all feeling in her fingers, she would touch something. Instinctively, she would try to close her hand around it and pull it towards the surface, but she never could. Her fingers were too numb and she was never strong enough. She would gasp for breath even though the frozen air felt like fire inside of her. Desperately, she would continue to try and try until finally, she always had to give up.

Spent and broken, she would lie sobbing on the cold, white ice and plead with every god in the universe to give her back her son. Time after time, she pleaded with them all to give her one more chance to make things different for him. She never asked that he be allowed to live—his illness would make that life unbearable. All she ever wanted was to be able to hold him and let him die in her arms.

Night after night, she lay on the ice as the cold crept up her arm and towards her heart. She knew she had to get up. She knew she had to get back inside and get warm again but whenever she tried to raise her arm, something would grab her wrist and hold her tight.

Every time it happened, she thought that it might just have been caught in the reeds or an underwater branch and every time she tried to wriggle it free. But it was never any use. It was stuck fast, and there was something else. The ice around had begun to buckle and the water began to rise, but it never startled her. Instead she always felt a dull sense of resignation and she allowed herself to be dragged under.

*

"You had that dream again last night, didn't you?" Mary asked as she bustled into the kitchen like a morning breeze, turning on all of the lights, the electric kettle, and turning up the thermostat. "I heard you cry out, you know. I went to see if you were alright, but you were sleeping again by the time I got there."

"What dream?" Gloria asked without turning from the window. That was where Mary always found her, and she had probably been standing there since the early hours of the morning.

"The same dream that you have been having for the last few weeks."

"And how would you know what I have been dreaming about?"

"Because I can hear you call his name every time you have it."

Gloria stiffened at that, but Mary was determined to push it a little further. "You know I am here for you when you are ready to sit down and talk about it."

"It's just a silly dream; there is nothing to talk about."

"As you wish," Mary decided to agree, for now, and made tea for the two of them. She didn't mention it, but she had been having her own recurring dream—a dream so vivid that it lingered for hours after she had woken.

It was always in the height of the summer and the kids were all there; Johnnie, Buddy, and their children, Joey and Susie, and Dwayne and Brad. C.C. was there too, smiling and laughing, and looking so relaxed. The sun was hot and its reflection was dancing on the lake, making golden ripples under the large blue sky.

Mary was sitting on the dock where she had often sat before, but somehow it all felt so different.

The younger kids were getting ready to go into the water and they were insisting that C.C. had to join them. After much cajoling, C.C. finally agreed on the condition that Buddy would come too. Buddy hesitated so Johnnie took her under one arm, and C.C. under the other, and began to wade out into the water. All of the kids squealed with laughter and followed, thrashing and splashing in the water as they went.

Mary's heart was dancing to the sounds of her family's laughter and she turned to where Gloria sat—but she wasn't there.

Then it dawned on Mary; she was sitting in what had long been Gloria's chair.

"I don't mean to go on and on about it," Mary ventured again after they had sat sipping their tea for a few minutes. She didn't want to be too pushy, but Gloria was clearly troubled and Mary felt more than duty-bound to try to do something about it. "But I do think that one of these days we will all have to sit down and talk about it."

"Talk about what, my dream?"

"Really Gloria? I am the one who is supposed to be evasive. You know very well that I don't mean that."

Gloria looked like she had been caught out and hesitated. It was happening more and more lately and, in an odd way, that made Mary feel better about herself. It didn't make her feel superior in any way, but it did make her feel more useful and less like a burden, and she needed to feel like that. And Gloria needed to realize something, too. Even though she would never admit it, she was reaching that stage of life where she needed looking after.

"I have given a great deal of thought to what you said about celebrating Christmas for the sake of my grandchildren," Mary continued with a growing sense of conviction and purpose. "And I am beginning to think it might be time that we got the whole family together for their sake. And it could allow the rest of us to begin to come to terms with all that happened."

"I see." Gloria asked and sat up straight as if she was steeling herself to face something she hadn't wanted to do. "But do you think the others would want to do that? Do you think they are ready?"

"Whether they are ready or not," Mary answered with as much conviction as she could muster. "I think it is something they need to do."

"Perhaps you are right," Gloria nodded, as if to herself. But even as she did, her face changed. "But are you sure that you are ready?"

"Yes, I believe I am."

She knew why Gloria had asked. In the first few years after Jake had left them, Mary had been in no mood to celebrate Christmas and Gloria had to step in. She had insisted that Mary and the children join her at the cottage and had done everything she could to make it as memorable and as magical as she could. Together with Johnnie, Buddy, and C.C., she had decorated every room. She'd had a neighbor string up

145

lights all around the cottage and all the way down to the boathouse, making everything look like something out of Santa's village.

At the time, Mary had resented her for that. She was lost in her hopelessness and was in no mood for the frivolity of Christmas. But as the years passed, she begrudgingly had to admit, at least to herself, that Gloria's Christmases had come to mean everything to her children. Since then she had gone along with it for that reason, but she had always done so with an air of martyrdom.

Since Jake had died, she had come to see how ridiculously self-indulgent that had been and it was embarrassing to her now. After a lifetime spent blaming him for everything, she had gone full-circle and now refused to allow herself to think even one single negative thought about him. She was not trying to make him into a saint, she was just trying to force herself to see him through the prism of her ongoing reformation.

He was, when all was said and done, the one who had really been aggrieved. She had seriously wronged him, and then she had lied to him and about him. But, when she was trying to be fair and honest with herself too, she had also realized there was no point in spending any more of her life beating up on herself about that. It had been what it had been and there was nothing she could do now but to try to undo some of the damage that had been caused by what should never have been allowed to happen. And to that end, she would now do whatever had to be done to make it possible for his children and grandchildren to remember him well.

"And I think it would be beneficial for all of us. It might allow us to find the closure we all need."

"And do you think the others might be ready for closure?" Gloria asked, but her voice was soft and distant—like she was really talking to herself.

"I think we have to find out. I think it is time we all got together."

"So, we should invite them for Christmas?"

"Well, at least some part of it."

"Very well, then," Gloria sighed and looked towards the window. "Perhaps you are right."

Mary followed her gaze and understood. "Gloria, what are you not telling me?"

Gloria slowly turned back and smiled a crooked little smile. "A great many things—as usual."

*

Mary nodded and decided to leave it at that, for now. She knew that Gloria had been taking calls from someone concerning Jake's estate, but she had chosen to keep the details to herself. At first, Mary had been a little miffed at that. A part of her felt entitled—as a widow—to at least know what was happening. But another part of her had insisted that she finally accept the fact that Jake had married again, and had raised another family in California. And she had to finally admit that he had honored all of his legal and moral requirements to her and her children.

Before, in her bouts of self-pity and self-justification, she had never given him the credit for that. He had always been more than generous in paying support, and alimony, and always paid on time and without stint. He had also set up a fund for her children to go to university. Johnnie and Buddy hadn't gone so C.C. had benefitted from it all. If Jake had any issue with that, he never mentioned it.

In her better days, when the spirit of positivity pulsed through her, Mary was quick to remind herself that she had no more claim on him or what he might have left behind. But in her heart, she hoped there might be something—some gesture to show that he had loved them all until the end.

She wanted to talk about those feelings, but Gloria was taciturn and spoke only of tangled legalities and filing the correct tax forms. Beyond that, she was not prepared to discuss the matter and Mary had to accept it.

The old Mary would have found a reason to be offended, but that would be so ungrateful. They were a well-off family who had been blessed with healthy and happy children, and grandchildren. In a world so full of suffering and strife, that was more than enough to be thankful for. Remembering all that she should be grateful for had become a morning ritual for her. It was how she focused her mind on becoming the person she now wanted to be.

It had been a struggle at first and it had been something that Gloria had been very quick to remind her of when she faltered, but not in a mean way. "You still have a family that loves you," she had mentioned whenever she caught Mary feeling sorry for herself.

"A family that wants nothing to do with me anymore?" Mary had complained, but that was more of a reflex. Deep down, she knew very well that it was not true. Her children were simply dealing with their own reactions, as well as giving her the time and space she needed to recover her composure.

Still, Mary had missed her family and the polite calls she made each week were never enough. When she had complained about that, Gloria had been quick to remind her that each one of her children also had their own issues to work through.

That made perfect sense, but it also touched a nerve. Mary had never allowed them to express their own feelings on everything that had happened. And it wasn't just because she had been ashamed; she was also a mother who had wanted to try to shield her children from the harsh truths of the world.

She had to force herself to remember all of that when Buddy rushed to get her off the phone. She was forthcoming with news of Dwayne and Brad, but beyond that she had little to say. She and Norm were fine, she would say and then ask after Gloria. She did ask how Mary was doing, too, but it was little more than a polite formality. And it was little more than Mary had any right to expect.

"Give her time," Gloria had advised when Mary had first complained about that. "Buddy hasn't stopped loving you."

"Then why can't she say that to me?"

"Probably because she has enough to do."

"Do you mean with Norm? I feel so bad about that. I was such a bad influence on her that way. She should have had a better role model." That was what she wanted to talk with Buddy about. She wanted to try to make amends for all of that, but clearly Buddy wasn't ready.

"Perhaps," Gloria had replied. "But I was thinking more about what it must be like with those little hell-raisers of hers."

It was probably meant to deflect her, but Mary had reacted impulsively. "Dwayne and Brad are angels; how dare you say such a thing."

*

Mary had immediately regretted her response. It was an old habit. She had always suspected that Gloria preferred Johnnie and Carol's children, especially Susie. They often talked on the phone, but Gloria rarely shared anything of what they talked about.

Despite all of her new resolutions, Mary couldn't help but be a little jealous of that. And, despite her better judgment, she had taken to eavesdropping. She was able to rationalize it by convincing herself that she was merely being vigilant for the sake of Gloria's health and well-being.

It didn't really help as she could only understand a little of what was being said. Over the last few years, Gloria and Susie seemed to have developed a connection that was deeper than words. It often made Mary feel left out. The last time they spoke, Mary decided to force the issue and walked right in as they were talking.

*

"I have to run now, Susie," Gloria said when she saw Mary. "Your grandmother has just come in."

Gloria listened to whatever the young girl was telling her and a brief smile lit up her face. "And I love you, too," Gloria responded and ended the call.

"Gathering information?" Mary smirked when Gloria slowly turned around to look at her.

"I was just talking with Susie, if you must know." Gloria said in her most off-handed manner, but it was clear that whatever she and Susie had been talking about had troubled her. "I find that she has the most remarkable insights for someone so young.

"Sometimes I think she and I must have been adopted," she added and tried to smile again, but it was a tired, sad smile.

Mary picked up on that and tried to play along. "In other words, she is your top spy?"

"You don't like Susie, do you?" Gloria asked.

It sounded more like a resigned declaration than an accusation, but Mary reacted without thinking. "What a terrible thing to say. I love all of my grandchildren."

"Of course you do, but you don't like Susie."

"Nonsense."

"Is it?"

"Well, if you must know," Mary conceded as there was little point in going head-to-head with Gloria when she was in one of these moods. "She reminds me far too much of you."

"And you don't like me either?"

"Oh, Gloria, why are we having this conversation?"

"Because our family is falling apart and I no longer have the strength to try to hold them together anymore."

Chapter 14

Because our family is falling apart and I no longer have the strength to try to hold them together anymore. Gloria's words had stayed with Mary and, along with her dream, it was becoming so glaringly obvious; it was going to fall to her to step up and try to bring the family together for Christmas. She wasn't ready for that. She was still trying to put her own life in order, but she had to. She was still a mother—and a grandmother; she had very little choice.

To make matters worse, since they had that talk, Gloria was getting worse by the day. She hardly seemed to sleep anymore. Most nights Mary heard her cry out: "Jake. Jake come back to me." It was a haunting sound, but by the time Mary got to her bedside Gloria was sleeping again. Fitfully, but Mary always decided against waking her.

Gloria was getting forgetful, too. She was misplacing her things and often got very impatient with herself. She got impatient with Mary once or twice, but caught herself quickly and apologized profusely. "Forgive me, Mary," she had said. "Please forgive me and don't leave me too."

Mary had become so concerned that she called the doctor. He was an old family friend and was willing to make the trek. He arrived late in the morning and insisted on seeing Gloria alone. They spoke in hushed voices and, even though Mary was standing just outside the door, she could hear little or nothing of what was said. She wasn't trying to pry; she was just concerned and did manage to scurry away and was waiting by the kitchen table when the doctor came down. He smiled an odd smile when she asked how Gloria was.

"Physically, she is as well as can be expected at her age," he answered. "But I suspect that recent events have taken a huge toll on her spirit. She is tired and, uncharacteristically for her, showing many of the symptoms of dysthymia, or chronic depression if you prefer."

"I see," Mary acknowledged. "And is there anything I should be doing to help her. Are there pills she should be taking?"

"There are, but I doubt she would take them. I have known Gloria for many years and she has always been a strong-minded individual. I doubt she would want to spend the rest of her days in some pharmaceutical haze. Is she still smoking pot?"

"Not so much," Mary told him. She had grown uncomfortable with it and Gloria had picked up on that. She never smoked in Mary's presence although she reeked of it when she came back from her visits to the island. "I might have discouraged her from that."

"I see. Well, in my opinion, it might be better than prescribing chemicals that she would have to get used to. I know this is not what you might expect to hear from a medical professional, but I say let her have her pot in peace. There is the matter of her glaucoma and it might just help her get past what is bothering her." He paused and looked out the window towards the island. He had been the one who had been called when Jake's body was found and he was the one who had recommended that the inquiry into the matter be quickly closed. "This winter must be particularly hard on her but I am sure that by the spring, she will be back to her old self."

"I hope so. Is there anything else I should be doing for her?"

The doctor smiled and shook his head slowly and deliberately. "This is Gloria's battle to fight but from what she tells me, you are already doing more than enough. She went as far as to say that she could not imagine how she would have managed without you. All I can add to that is to say: Keep it up.

"Though there is one thing that might be of help," he mentioned casually as he put on his coat and prepared to go back out into the cold. "She spoke to me about the possibility of having the family come together for Christmas. I realize," he paused like he was selecting his words. "That it might present some difficulties—logistically speaking—but I think it would do her the world of good."

"Of course," Mary agreed even as her mind began to wander through the difficulties it might present. "But there must be something else I can do—in the meantime?"

"Keep her in tea and good company," the doctor advised and smiled again. "From what she has told me, she would be in a far worse state of mind if it wasn't for you."

Those words warmed Mary's heart as she stood by the screen door and watched the doctor's car as he carefully turned and drove away. The driveway had been ploughed, but there were still quite a few icy patches.

After she had gone back inside and made tea, and brought some up to Gloria who agreed to stay in bed for a while, Mary sat down and thought about what she must do. She would have to call one of her children. She just couldn't decide which one.

Johnnie would drop everything and come running, but Mary was reluctant to do that. Gloria had told her what Susie had said about Carol wanting him to take a break from his family. She would not have meant it for something like this, but Mary still wanted to respect her wishes. She and Carol had not always seen eye to eye and Mary wanted to avoid doing anything to make things worse.

Buddy would drop everything, too, but that hardly seemed fair. Before, Mary had made far too many demands on her and had never given her the time to sort her own life out. From what Gloria had heard, poor Buddy was paying the price for that now.

That just left C.C. and Mary had no idea how she could even begin to broach it with her.

C.C. picked up her phone, but she hesitated again. She wished she hadn't agreed to do it, but she had and she just had to get on with it. *Just pretend it's a sales call*, she reminded herself as she made her third attempt. *Why is it so hard to talk with your own mother?*

She wished she hadn't asked herself that; it released a barrage of reasons so she called before any of them had time to settle in. "Hi, Mom. I was just calling to see how you are doing, and to apologize for not calling before. Things have been a bit hectic with the promotion and all."

"C.C.? Now this is a wonderful surprise."

It was probably just a reflex response, but C.C. had to stop herself from reading anything into it. "So, how have you been?"

"I have been very well, dear, thanks for asking, and may I offer my belated congratulations on your big promotion. Gloria and I were so proud when we heard."

"Thanks, Mom, and how is Gloria doing?"

"Well she is not doing so well. In fact, we just had the doctor pop in to see her."

"Oh, and why was that?"

"Well, she hasn't really been right since Jake died. It's understandable, of course, but I think she might be getting a bit lost in herself."

"Really?"

"Yes. She is starting to forget things. She leaves her glasses somewhere and can't remember where. The number of times I have to search the whole house—not that I am complaining. I am more than happy to do it. But she is always leaving her teacups around; it is so unlike her. Sometimes, I wonder if she isn't getting a bit confused."

"You know I was talking with Susie the other day and she was saying the same thing."

"Well, I am not sure how she would know. Nobody has been up to see us since . . . well, you know."

"Everyone has just been busy, Mom. You know how things can get."

"I do, dear, but it would do Gloria a world of good to see you all again."

"Well, that's another reason I called. I was thinking I might take a drive up there this weekend."

"Oh, C.C., that would be lovely, but are you sure? It's very snowy up here and that car of yours is not made for that type of driving."

"I know, Mom, that's why I was thinking of asking Johnnie if I could borrow his truck. And, I might bring Susie along."

"That's wonderful news, dear, and it will be so nice to have you here, but are you sure that bringing Susie is wise? I would think that she would be far too busy with her school work, and all."

"She is going through a bit of a rough time, right now, and spending time with Gloria might be just what the doctor ordered—and seeing you too, of course."

"Well, I am sure Gloria will be delighted to see both of you."

C.C. had to end the call at that; she had a call waiting, but she was happy with herself.

That feeling stayed with C.C. for the rest of the afternoon and right through the evening. Even when she thought about it with her "business head," it still made sense. She was the one who had to step up. Buddy and Johnnie were still dealing with the loss of their father; she wasn't. She was sad for him, but he wasn't hers to grieve.

And her mother had lost her husband—even if they had been divorced for years. It was now so obvious that Mary had never stopped loving him. All the stuff she used to say about how bad he was, and all the terrible things he had done to her . . . it was all just the bullshit Mary used to cover up that she was the one who had messed up. C.C. had been the same when she and Michele had split up.

All of that aside, it was Gloria who needed her the most right now. She had lost her only child, and she had watched it happen right in front of her. She was in no fit state to pull the others together, but C.C. was.

Mindful of what happened at the school, she decided to call Carol first and she did it as soon as she got to the office, right after she had checked the west coast figures. There was a slight uptick, but they were still going to fall short.

"Hi, Sis," she offered as cheerfully and as off-handed as she could. With everything that was going on she expected Carol to be a bit frazzled.

"Hi, C.C., what's up?"

"Well, I have been thinking and I wanted to run something by you."

"Oh? Should I assume this has to do with family matters?"

"Yes, does that surprise you?"

"Just that you would call me beforehand."

"You're not going to let that one drop, are you?"

"Not until the next time you screw things up for me."

"Fair enough, but here's the thing. I was thinking of driving up to see Mom and Gloria on the weekend, and I was wondering if I could take Susie along?"

"I take it that you guys have already talked about this?"

"Yup."

"And she has told you about the ongoing cold war between your brother and Joey?"

"She has. I thought that a few days with Gloria might be helpful."

"Leaving you and your mother to do what?"

"Mary and I are okay, these days."

"Have you even talked to her since Jake died?"

"Hey, I just talked with her yesterday."

"I do hope you know what you are doing."

"So, is that a yes?"

"It's up to Susie, but I would like to make a suggestion. How would you feel about taking your brother, too? He could use a trip to the cottage right now, and it would give Joey and me a few days on our own."

"I don't mind. If he wants to come, then sure."

"Okay then, there's just one more thing. I want you to call and ask him."

"Why?"

"Because he never says no to you."

"What can I say?"

C.C. ended the call and felt even better about herself. She knew that Carol, for all of her kidding around, was happy about it all. Susie would be delighted and Johnnie never needed an excuse to go to the cottage.

She was still in a good mood when one of the senior reps called to tell her that they were about to lose a major account. C.C. had heard about it, but had decided to wait for the rep to call her. "How bad is it?" she asked while bringing up the client's account on her screen.

"Pretty bad," the rep answered nervously. "I've been trying everything I could think of, but I can't seem to get through to them."

"I see," C.C. stalled as she checked a few other screens. "What reason did they give you?" she finally asked.

"I can't get a straight answer on that. One minute it is price but when I moved on that, it became quality. When I tried to sound that out it became about a better deal from someone else."

"I see," C.C. repeated after a pause. Steve was one of the guys who had given her a hard time when she was in the field. He had been number one until she came along and he had never gotten over that. She used to spend time fantasying about how she would get even with him but now, as she had him by the balls, she realized she was past all of that. "You do know they are being taken over?" she asked in a calm voice.

"No, I didn't."

She was tempted to ask him why not, but she didn't. Instead she just tapped her fingers on her desk, loud enough for him to hear.

"So, what should I do?" he asked, hesitantly.

"Leave it with me for now," she answered through a smile. "I'll make a few calls."

She already had. The take-over had just been agreed and the new parent company was holding the announcement until the beginning of the new year, but C.C. hadn't waited. She knew some people there and tracked down the Purchasing Manager—Sandra, an old friend from university. C.C. had already taken her for lunch and had turned on the charm.

It had worked. Sandra had signed agreements for the next two years, but C.C. wasn't ready to share any of that with Steve. Instead, she would send him over when the new deal went through. She would warn him that Sandra was a ball-buster who had no time for the old school guys and that he'd better bring his 'A' game. She would tip Sandra off too. They had always enjoyed a few laughs and she would be more than happy to play along. It was a bit mean of her, but it was what Steve needed. The world had changed and he needed to evolve with it. She was still smiling to herself when she called her brother.

"S'up, Sis?"

"You sound very chipper."

"Yeah, I finally managed to get some work done this morning. One of the painters is off sick."

"Sounds like you could use an apprentice."

"Don't you start."

"Okay, okay. Listen. I was thinking of heading up to see Mom and Gloria this weekend."

"Why?"

"Because I am a good daughter who cares about her family."

"Since when?"

"Since you became an asshole that doesn't."

"Oh, piss off. I get enough grief at home; I don't need you piling on."

"Then don't pull the tiger's tail. Anyhow. I was calling to see if you would let me borrow the truck. The Barbie car might get lost in the snow. You can tag along, if you like."

"It does sound like a good idea—even if it is coming from you. Let me check with Carol."

"No need, I already did."

"Oh?"

"Yup, you, me, and Susie are going to Grandma's house in the woods."

"Sounds great, but I got to ask: what are you really up to?"

"You'll find out when we get there."

Chapter 15

The morning after C.C.'s call, Mary stood by the kitchen window. Gloria was up and about again and had insisted on going over to the island. Mary had raised a token resistance, but Gloria told her that the doctor had said that it was important that she maintain her daily routines. She also said that he had said that it would help to keep her motivated. Mary couldn't argue with any of that so she offered to go with her, but Gloria wouldn't hear of it.

"You do far too much for me already," she argued. "I couldn't possible ask you to watch over me every minute of the day. You have enough to do and besides, the doctor was telling me that I must do whatever I can to retain my independence. Apparently, recent studies have said that it can be of critical importance when fighting off chronic depression."

"So, you have accepted that as the prognosis?" Mary asked kindly. Gloria seemed better than she had in a while.

"I have because the alternatives would be far too depressing."

Mary couldn't argue with that, either. Gloria was putting on her bravest face.

"Very well, then. But don't stay out too long." She conceded, but she would keep watch from the window. The ice was solid, but Gloria could easily slip and fall. Left unnoticed, she could freeze to death in next to no time.

It was a fine, bright day. A brilliant, cold sun beamed down from the deep blue sky and Mary could see Gloria's breath on the air. She was talking to herself—or Jake—and that seemed to be bringing her some peace. Then, after a few quick glances towards the cottage, Gloria moved to where she thought she couldn't be seen and took a few puffs from her pipe. That brought a smile to Mary's face. The older Gloria got, the more childlike she became.

But whatever benefit Gloria had gotten from her walk, and her pipe, seemed to be wearing off as she made her way back. Perhaps it was being stuck in the cottage. Perhaps she needed to get away from it for a while. Maybe, in January, Mary would try to organize a week in the sun, or a cruise, but in the meantime, she had the news of C.C.'s call.

Gloria did perk up for a moment when Mary told her, but she soon sagged into her chair and asked Mary if she would make tea for them.

"I thought you would be happier," Mary prodded after she had returned with the tea.

"Oh, I am, Mary. Or as happy as these short days will allow." She turned to look towards the window and sighed. "I don't remember a winter having such an effect on me before. But," she turned back and looked at Mary. "We mustn't let anybody know about that. It must be our little secret."

"Oh, I am sure that you will feel much better about everything when you see Johnnie and C.C. again, and, of course, Susie."

Gloria smiled briefly. "I do hope you are right." She seemed to dwell on that for a moment, but then began to look worried again. "Are you sure it is a good idea to have them drive all the way up here to see me like this?"

"Then we will just have to make sure that you are well rested between now and then."

"I am sure you are right, Mary. And thank you. I don't know how I would manage without you."

They settled into a silence after that, sipping their tea as the afternoon ticked away, growing darker and colder as it did. The furnace came on and the rumbling and gusting of warmer air was a welcome distraction. Inactivity did not sit well with Mary; it gave her too much time to think. But she had to sit and think and she had to think about Gloria. How much longer could the old woman last? And what would become of them all in the vacuum her passing would leave?

When the darkness had settled on the lake, Mary rose and turned on the lamp. Gloria had fallen asleep so she quietly took the cups to the sink and rinsed them. She would make a light supper for both of them and pack Gloria off to bed early. She could take a book up with her and curl up while Mary made plans for when the others visited.

She would have to do some shopping as there would be five mouths to feed. That would mean a trek down to the stores. Or she could ask Johnnie and C.C. to pick up the things they needed. Yes, that would be better. If she went to the stores, then Gloria would insist on coming too and she needed to rest.

She hoped Susie would not be too much for Gloria. Maybe she should have a word with Johnnie about that. Or she could mention it to C.C., she seemed to be in one of her "organizing moods."

She started to make lists because she was nervous. It would be the first time she would spend a weekend with any of her family since Jake had died. So much had happened so quickly back then that she never had the chance to have a proper talk about it all. Everybody had rushed off back to the city and, while she was happy about that at the time, she now realized; they should have stayed and talked about it and she should have been the one who made sure they did.

They would have to do it now and they would have to talk about everything. She felt the first fluttering of panic in her stomach and despite her earlier misgivings, she wished Buddy was coming with them.

Johnnie had just finished cleaning off the paint brushes when Buddy texted him. She was nearby and wanted to know if he had time for coffee and, of course, a few donuts. He did. He had finished what had to be done and, if he said so himself, it looked pretty damned good. The walls were a hunter's green and the trim was a smoky white. It hadn't looked so good when he had seen the color cards, but now it looked fine. And most importantly, the client was happy— and that was unusual. She was one of those people who could never make up her mind. *Be there in ten*, he responded and cleaned his hands as well as he could. He was a good painter, but he always ended up with paint under his nails.

Buddy had the coffees and donuts on the table when he arrived. Christmas jingles filled the coffee shop and almost brightened the dull afternoon. "I just got them," she smiled. "They're still hot."

"The donuts?"

She smiled at that, but it was a brittle smile. He could tell that she was holding things together, but only barely.

"So," he asked with as much nonchalance as he could manage. "Anything new?"

"Not a lot. I did some shopping for the kids—for Christmas. I am trying to get in the mood for it, but . . . well, you know. With so much hanging in the air, I have decided that the best thing I can do is to go on like everything is normal and wait to see what happens next."

"It's probably for the best," Johnnie agreed and started in on his first donut.

"Is it?"

"I think so."

"So, you are not going to tell me?"

"Tell you what?"

"What you and Norm talked about the other night."

"You know the rules of boys' night out."

"I thought that was Fight Club."

"Same thing, really."

She tried to smile at that, but she was too worried. He knew her well enough to be able to read the signs.

"Listen, Bud. All I can tell you is that you shouldn't be too concerned. Norm has got some stuff he has to get through, but it's nothing to do with you."

"I know you mean well, Johnnie, but that is not very helpful. What am I supposed to think? That he has some major health issue or something?"

"It's more of a something kind of thing."

"Meaning?"

"Meaning that he asked me not to tell you."

"So, you do know?"

"I do." He wanted to leave it at that, but he couldn't. She was his kid sister and he couldn't do that to her. Besides, she was making that face. "Listen, Bud. Norm is losing his job. The whole office is being shut down. He didn't want you to know until he had found something else."

She took a few moments to absorb that and while she did, she sipped from her coffee. She seemed relieved for a moment and then she looked worried again. He decided to stay silent and let her deal with it whatever way she had to. He watched her as he finished his donut and reached for another while in the background, the Christmas jingles played on regardless.

"Why couldn't he have just told me that?" she finally asked and Johnnie could tell, she was about to start feeling sorry for herself again.

"Maybe he didn't want you to be worried." But it was more than that. Johnnie understood. Norm had always been the butt of so many family jokes. His job, and his ability to provide for his family, was the one thing nobody could ever take from him, up until now.

"Are you going to be alright?" he asked after his sister had sat in silence for a while.

"Of course," she answered and straightened herself. "Now that you have finally told me what the real problem is."

"Are you going to tell him that you know?"

"Don't you think I should, or would that violate your sacred Bro-code?

"You know," she continued as she started to wind herself up. "I think you should have told me the moment you found out and not have me stewing for all this time. I didn't know what to think and you . . .," she pointed at him, but her words trailed off. She began to sob, silently.

Johnnie sat and watched her. He was torn between wanting to reach out to her and wanting to stay the hell out of it. There was nothing he could do for Norm, and past experience had taught him there was little he could do for Buddy when she got into one of these moods. Instead, he ate another donut and thought about what a pile of shit his life really was.

"By the way," he added after they had sat in silence for too long. "C.C., Susie and I are taking a trip up to the cottage this weekend." He wasn't sure if he should tell her, but she was going to find out, sooner or later.

"Oh? When was that decided?"

"The other day. It's all very last minute."

"I see. And did anyone stop to think that I might like to be included?"

"I guess we thought you had enough on your plate."

"I see, and was this Mom's idea?"

"I don't think so. C.C. called her the other day and then decided to visit."

"C.C. called Mom?"

"Like I said."

"I wonder what she's up to?"

"Maybe she is just trying to make peace with the past. I don't know."

"C.C.? Making peace with the past?"

"Could happen."

"And Mom is okay with this?"

"Sounds like it. I think Gloria is not doing so well and Mom feels that a visit might help."

"And Norm and I were not supposed to know?"

"I just told you."

"I see. And while we are sharing information, I should tell you something."

"What?"

"Oh, it's probably nothing, but you should have a little chat with your wife about her lunch dates."

She stormed out before Johnnie could say anything, but she started to berate herself on the way home. Why did she have to go and say that to him? It was just mean and spiteful. It was one of those times when she couldn't help herself; it was out of her mouth before she realized.

Neural networks, she reminded herself. It was another one of her bad habits. Whenever she was hurt, she would lash out and do something stupid. Something that would only make things worse.

She regretted it, of course, and now she would have to try to make amends. She would call Johnnie and tell him why she had said what she had said. Then she would call Carol, too, and try to explain it to her.

Johnnie would probably let it go at that, but Carol? This might be a tough one for her to step over. Especially if there really was something going on.

After thinking about that for a while, she tried to tell herself that if there was something going on, then it was better that Johnnie knew about it. Just like she should have been told about what was going on with Norm.

That was it in a nutshell. That was why she had felt so hurt, and why she had lashed out. She should have been told. She should not have been left to worry in the dark. Johnnie should have told her. Norm should have told her. She should not have been left to worry herself sick that it was something she had done.

But, then again, maybe it was something she had done. Maybe that was why her own husband did not feel that he could come to her when his world was falling apart.

When she got to the school, she had to put all of that aside. She would come back to it later but for now, she had to be a different person—for the kid's sake. She had to be what a mother had to be; calm and serene, wise and patient, and attentive to every little inflection and nuance. The kids were not so oblivious. They knew things weren't right at home. Kids always noticed things like that.

She managed it very well and she was careful not to over-indulge them. She listened to everything they had to say about their day. She went through their bags and asked if they had enjoyed the snacks she had packed for them. She made them supper and let them go and watch some T.V.—but only for an hour. They could pick one show each and after that she would read to them until they fell asleep. Norm would be late, as usual. He said he had to stay late at the office, but that made no sense now.

A hundred thoughts flashed across her mind, but one lingered within her. The poor guy was embarrassed and was trying to stay away from her. But that was good. That was something she could do something about.

While the kids watched their shows, she took a steak from the freezer. She had been saving it for a special occasion. She had potatoes that would be perfect roasted. She had sour cream and chives, and, she smiled to herself, she had a bottle of his favorite wine.

She thought about getting dressed up, but decided against it. She wanted it to be a different kind of evening. She wanted it to be about communication; open and honest communication. She wanted him to know that he could talk to her about the problems he was facing. She wanted him to know that they were a team that could face anything together.

She texted him to make sure he wouldn't stop for something to eat on the way home.

Let me know when you'll be home and I will have dinner ready.

"Are we not going to have Christmas this year?" Dwayne asked from the doorway. Buddy had no idea how long he had been standing there.

"Oh, sweetie." She walked towards him and knelt down so she could hold him tightly. "Of course we are. Why would you ask such a thing?"

"Because," Dwayne stammered as he struggled with his emotions. "You and Daddy have not even talked about it once."

Chapter 16

"I don't think we should talk about all of that right now," Johnnie muttered with a quick nod in the direction of Susie. She was in the seat behind them and had her headphones on, but C.C. wasn't going to let it go so easily.

"Don't worry about her, she can handle it, and it's not like she doesn't know what's going on."

"I still don't want to talk about all that stuff. I just want to get away from it all for a few days."

"And you will. As soon as we get to Grandma's house you can go out and play with your little toys in the snow."

They had been talking about the situation with Joey and all he had managed to do was to make it clear to both of them that he had no idea what to do next. Joey had dug his heels in and was refusing to go back to school and he and Carol were not on the same page about that. But even as he tried to explain his side of the story, he could hear it. He was coming across like a stubborn mule and C.C. was not the type to let something like that slide. She was going to have it out with him.

"Why not just let him try it for a while and if he doesn't like it, he can go back and finish school. At least that way, he would know." C.C. was more determined than usual. After her escapade at the school, she probably felt like she owed them one.

"Can't you just leave it alone?"

"Have you ever known me to able to leave anything alone?" She was pushing him, but that wasn't unusual. That had always been their pattern.

"What about this whole, new you?" he asked. "What about all these changes you have been telling me about? Because you sound the same to me."

"Right there," C.C. laughed. "The old me would have taken that personally, but the new me knows that you are just trying to avoid the issue. Just let the kid make his choice. What's the big deal with that?"

Johnnie sighed and stared at the road ahead. Driving to the cottage in the winter was a breeze. Traffic was light and the roads had been ploughed, but he still had to pay attention in those spots where blowing snow had drifted over and blurred the markings.

"What is the real deal, Johnnie?"

"The real deal is that work is drying up."

"Work is always drying up. You have been through this before."

"And that is why I don't want my kids to have to go through it."

"That's just bullshit. No matter what your kids decide to do, they are going to have to deal with whatever crap life throws at them. And, believe me, what they are being taught at school isn't going to be of much help. Besides, any clown can get a degree these days. What we really need are people who actually know how to build things. Just look at what StatsCan are saying: there is a shortage of skilled labor. Anybody with a business head would say that is where the opportunities are."

"And anybody who is actually in this business knows that nobody wants to pay for skilled labor anymore."

They had been underbid on two more jobs in the last week, alone. Carol had broken the news to him without comment. In a way, it almost seemed like she was happy about it—that it was playing into something she had been planning. He had thought about having that out with her, but he wasn't sure. What Buddy had said to him was a part of it, but he knew better than to react to anything she said. Buddy always lashed out like that when things were going wrong for her. But if there was something going on . . . Shit! As if he didn't have enough to deal with.

"Okay. Let me try again. What's the real issue here, Johnnie?"

"That's the only issue, as far as I am concerned."

"And what is that; that you can't handle a bit of competition?"

"You know," he looked over at her. "I think I preferred you when you didn't give a damn about anybody else."

"That's so sweet of you to say, but it doesn't answer my question."

He took a quick glance over his shoulder. Susie was still listening to something and staring out the window. He looked back at C.C. and grimaced a little. "Well, if you must know."

"I do."

"I just can't see my way forward anymore."

"Where you ever able to see it?"

"Maybe not, but before I could see what was right in front of me. You know, get some work, do it properly, get some money, pay the bills and be happy for a few moments."

"So, what has changed?"

"Everything; me, Carol, the kids, the world. It seems like only a few days ago that Carol and I were just starting out and everything was obvious. We would get a house and start a family. Our kids would grow up to be happy and find their own way in the world, and one day we would get to sit on the dock and look back at it all and smile."

"Ah, that's so cute. But why would you think that Gloria would leave the cottage to you?"

"Because I am her favorite. But now, when I look forward, I don't see any of that anymore."

"What do you see?"

He turned and looked directly at her. "I see myself, sitting alone, staring into the water and wondering what the hell it was all supposed to be about."

When they got to the cottage, Mary was standing in the enclosed part of the veranda anxiously waiting to greet them. She was warm and welcoming before she hurried them all inside. The sun had set and the evening was going to be another cold one. Once they had taken off their coats, she made her usual fuss and insisted that they must eat something. She had made soup and sandwiches because she wasn't sure what time they were coming. C.C. had told Gloria, but she had gone for a nap without telling Mary, and she hadn't surfaced yet.

Johnnie was surprised by that and asked if he should check on her but Mary said no; she had just checked before they arrived. She also told them about the doctor's visit and that Gloria didn't want them to be concerned. "Should we be concerned?" Johnnie asked when C.C. and Susie went to put the groceries away.

"Well . . .," Mary answered. "She is having a bit of trouble dealing with you know what. And she has been having trouble sleeping, and I think she has let herself get a bit run down."

Johnnie might have said more, but C.C. came back and cut him off. "Maybe she shouldn't be taking her naps so late in the afternoon? Anyway, we're all here to try to cheer her up." She was in one of her take-control moods and led Johnnie back to the kitchen where Susie had been waiting.

They ate even though they were not that hungry—they had stopped for burgers and fries on the way, but they knew not to mention that. And while they ate, Mary chatted on, asking after each one in turn, and then after the rest of the family.

When Gloria did come down, she looked at them all like she was confused. "I didn't realize that you were coming today," she explained as Mary and C.C. exchanged glances. "But it's a wonderful surprise." She greeted Johnnie and C.C. warmly and then held out her arms as Susie rushed towards her and they hugged for the longest time.

After they had finished eating, they moved into the other room. The woodstove had been lit and it was so warm and inviting. Johnnie had brought in more logs too, so they wouldn't have to budge for the rest of the evening. After adding to the fire, he sat in the deep armchair and soon nodded off. Susie and Gloria sat by the small table and played cards while Mary and C.C. sat opposite each other, nodding and smiling whenever they made eye contact.

"You're looking great, Mom," C.C. said after they had sat for a while. "You have lost so much weight."

"I will take that as a compliment and not as a comment on how I must have looked before."

"I would, if I were you," Gloria joined in. "Our C.C. was never one to be overly generous with her compliments."

"And what's that supposed to mean?" C.C. asked, pretending to glare at Gloria.

"Yeah," Susie sided with her. "She is always complimenting me."

"That's because you deserve it," Gloria laughed and squeezed Susie's hand.

"Actually," C.C. corrected her. "It is because I happen to believe in giving credit where it is due."

Susie beamed with pride while Gloria pretended to study her cards. "What's seldom is wonderful," she muttered just loud enough for everyone to hear.

"Oh my god," C.C. groaned and looked at Mary. "Don't you just love when this family gets together."

"Actually, I do, and tomorrow we must sit down and talk about Christmas."

C.C. made a point of being the first one up and it wasn't just because she was on a mission; she had really enjoyed sitting with her mother the night before. In fact, she had enjoyed being with all of them. It felt like the way family was supposed to feel and it made her think that they could do Christmas at the cottage, again. They hadn't in years. Part of it was her. She had gone away to college and was never in the mood for it and then the others started families and the trek was too much for them. Gloria had taken it as well as she could and had spent Christmas in the city with them, but it was never the same.

C.C. would be up for it as she had not made other plans as yet. They hadn't discussed it yet, but Heather would most likely go to her parents. And she still hadn't told them about C.C..

Buddy may or may not be a bit of a problem—depending on how things were going with Norm. If there was a problem, C.C. decided, she could always have a little chat with him.

Carol might be more difficult, but if C.C. could just get Johnnie to agree to let Joey do his thing then there would be one less issue. It could all work, she decided as the kettle was just coming to the boil.

"You are looking very pleased with yourself." Mary remarked as she walked to the light switch, but C.C. had already turned them all on.

"Oh. Hi Mom, yes, I am. I had forgotten how nice it is being up here in the winter." She smiled and walked over and took her mother in her arms. "And it's nice being here with you."

Mary got a bit flustered and tried to wriggle free, muttering something about having to get breakfast ready for the others, but C.C. didn't let her go. "I mean it, Mom."

"I know you do, dear and I really appreciate it."

C.C. gave her one more hug and loosened her arms. "And now, if you don't mind, I have decided that I am going to make breakfast for everyone."

Mary smiled away the little tears that were forming in the corners of her eyes. "My dear, I want you to always know that I am so proud of you, and all that you have done with your career and all, but I am sorry to have to tell that when it comes to cooking . . . well, you are the living proof that women can't have it all."

"You know, Mom, when you say things like that, I know I really am your daughter."

C.C. was being flippant, but it caused her mother to hesitate. "C.C.? Do we need to talk about . . . well, you know?"

"Oh, that? That's old news now, Mom. We've all moved on from that."

"Have we?"

"Yes, we all have new and far more complicated problems these days."

They were still laughing at that when Johnnie made his way down. "What the hell are you two cackling about?"

"Mom and I are having a moment, if you don't mind. There's coffee over there." C.C. pointed with a spatula and dripped egg spots all over the floor.

"Perhaps, I should take over the eggs," Mary suggested as she wiped up the mess. "And you can butter the toast."

"Mom! I was doing fine until that big jerk came along."

"It's payback, Sis."

"For what?"

"Buddy and I were doing fine until you came along."

"Mom! Did you hear what he just said to me?"

"Now children," Mary tried to admonish them, but she couldn't keep a straight face.

"What's going on?" Susie asked from the doorway, like she was unsure if she should intrude.

*

After Gloria had joined them, and they had all eaten, it was decided: Johnnie would go to the store and pick up a few washers for the dripping tap in the second washroom, as well as new filters for the furnace, a new snow shovel as the old one had cracked, and a case of beer for himself.

C.C. would take Gloria across to the island and Susie would stay with Mary. Susie might have wanted to go with Gloria, but no one thought that would be right. So, C.C. bundled up in her mother's coat and boots and trekked off with her grandmother clutching her arm.

Gloria was hunched over as she carefully chose each step. She had been back and forth so often that she had made a smooth path through the thick snow, a smooth path that was packed down and now very slippery. C.C. walked to the side, in the deeper snow. It was tough going, but it allowed her to keep her balance and offer support when Gloria seemed like she might fall. It took a while, but they got there.

At Gloria's urging, they moved around the edge of the island, out of sight of the cottage. There in the deep snow lay the frozen flowers that Gloria and Mary had left; brightly colored things lying in the great whiteness. When they got to where the shore line began, they stood in silence looking down at them. They stood together but apart as they each dealt with their own thoughts.

In time, Gloria had to rest so C.C. dusted off a rock and Gloria sat and smiled up at her. "I hope you don't mind, but I am going to have a few puffs of my pipe. Mary doesn't like me smoking it in the house, so I come over here to do it. And it helps me find some peace." She took a few hits and offered the pipe to C.C..

"No, I'm okay," C.C. shook her head. "But how are you really doing? Mom says she is a bit concerned about you."

Gloria looked at her for a few moments and slowly exhaled. "Your mother always has to be concerned with something."

"Maybe, but she said that you had the doctor over to see you. Is there anything you are not telling us?"

"A great many things."

"Gloria?"

"What?"

"You know very well what."

"Oh, don't be such a fuss pot. I am doing well enough but what I want to know is; how is Johnnie doing?"

"He's alright. Why do you ask?"

"Because of what Jake asked him to do. I can't for the life of me understand what made him do it. Obviously, he wasn't thinking clearly."

C.C. said nothing and listened as Gloria told her the whole story, her old, wrinkled face contorting as she relayed the pain and suffering of her son, and her grandson. She spoke solemnly and slowly until her voice began to quaver as she relived those terrible moments when Jake's canoe finally left her sight, only to return a few minutes later, empty. C.C. reached out and took her grandmother's hands in hers. It was all beginning to make sense now. No wonder Johnnie hadn't been the same since.

"And you, Gloria. Will you be okay?" She asked as she brushed back a few grey wisps from the old woman's face.

"Why would you ask such a thing?" Gloria smiled and fought back her tears. "I will be fine—or as fine as someone my age has any right to expect. But there are a few more things we need to talk about."

Chapter 17

After watching C.C. and Gloria make their way across the lake, Mary turned back to the table and began to tidy up. Susie, who had been watching her watch the others, insisted on helping and Mary was happy about that. "So?" she asked as they began to clear off the table together. "How is school?"

"It's okay."

"Just okay? I have always heard about what a bright young lady you are and how well you do at school. Don't be so modest about that. I am sure you work very hard for it."

"Oh, that part is fine. It's all the other stuff."

"Do you mean boys?"

Susie blushed a little and smiled to herself. "Yeah, boys, and all the other stuff."

"Like?"

"Well," Susie looked at her and seemed to be deciding what to say. "It's like all the other kids are pretending to be so much older than they are. Nobody wants to just be a kid anymore. Everyone wants to be all grown up and have all these grown up problems."

"That sounds terrible, and very foolish."

"I think so, but nobody else agrees with me."

"Nobody?"

"Well . . . none of my friends."

"And your brother?

"It's okay," Mary added when Susie hesitated. "Gloria has told me all about it."

"Yeah," Susie nodded and looked relieved. "He's changed so much."

"Boys do at his age."

"But you don't understand, Granny. He says all these dark, terrible things and that scares me."

"Things like . . .?"

"Well, he says that the whole world is coming to an end—you know, because of the environment—and nobody is really doing anything about it."

"I see."

"And he says things like 'all adults are screwed in the head.' He even says that about Mom and Dad."

"I see. And have you talked with your mom and dad about all this?"

"A bit, but they are both so busy. I don't want to bother them."

"Well, I think if they realized how much it bothered you, they would find the time to talk with you. This is not the sort of thing a young lady of your age should have to go through alone. Isn't there anybody else you can talk with?"

"I used to talk with Gigi, but lately . . . I don't know. It seems like I'm just bothering her, too."

"Oh, Susie. Please don't ever think of it that way. There are things happening in Gloria's life, but they have nothing to do with you. If anything, you are the greatest joy she still has."

Susie seemed happy with that for a moment, but then looked so concerned.

"Is Gigi dying?"

"Of course not," Mary answered instinctively. "But she is having a few issues that are not uncommon for people her age. She is quite old, you know, and at her age life becomes a little harder. But she is still . . . quite content, most of the time. And she did get so excited when I told her you were coming."

That had a positive impact on Susie, so Mary decided to raise the subject. "And if you can help me to get everyone to agree, we could all spend Christmas up here. I am sure that would make her very, very happy."

"I did ask my dad about it." Susie ventured.

"And what did he say?"

"He said he would talk with Mom, but then all the stuff with Joey started and now no one seems to want to talk about it."

"I see. It is understandable, but it would be a shame if we didn't. Perhaps it is time to talk with your mother?"

"I want to, but she is so busy all the time."

"Too busy for Christmas? I wouldn't think so."

"Maybe you could talk with them?"

"I could, but I might not be the best person to do it. I think you should get your Aunt C.C. to do it. She knows how to get your father to do anything."

"Yeah, my mom always says that too."

"We used to have wonderful Christmases up here," Mary sighed. She had been part of the reason they had stopped coming. She had made it seem that it was about trekking the children up, but it wasn't. She had been jealous of Gloria and the wonderful times they had. "Really wonderful."

"My dad used to tell me about them and he always smiled when he did."

"Then it is settled," Mary decided and smiled. "Susie?"

"Yes, Granny?"

"Could I ask a favor of you? Could you let me be a bigger part of your life?

"I know that before," she added when Susie didn't respond, "it might have seemed that I didn't care for you as much as I should have, but you have to understand something about me. I was not well. In many ways it was like what you were saying about the other kids at school. I became obsessed with all that was wrong in my life and could not see what was right. I am not sure if you can understand what I mean by that, but what I really want you to know is that I am getting better now and I want to show you the love that you deserve."

Susie rose and stood in front of her. Already she was taller than Mary. She reached forward with her arms and they hugged like they had never hugged before. "I would really like that," she whispered against her grandmother's greying head.

"Good," Mary agreed as she stepped back and tried to regain her compose. Standing in her granddaughter's embrace, she had felt that her heart would melt into a puddle on the floor. "And as for your brother, I am going to tell you that you mustn't worry about him. He is a fine young man who is just going through that teenage stage that boys have to go through, but don't be concerned. He will come through it and he will become a better man because of it."

"Did my daddy go through something like that?"

"Your father," Mary laughed. "Was a right little hell-raiser in his day."

"Oh, really?"

"Oh, yes. I could tell you some stories."

"You could, but you won't," C.C. interjected from the doorway. She and Gloria had come in quietly.

"And as for your Aunt C.C.," Mary continued with a huge smile on her face. "What that girl put me through . . . Isn't that right, Gloria?"

"I have no idea what you mean," Gloria responded and turned away before they could see the smile on her face.

"And what the hell is going on in here?" Johnnie asked from the back door as he stomped his feet on the mat to shake off the snow. "Or should I ask?"

"No!" Mary, C.C., and Susie answered in an almost perfect unison.

∗

With Johnnie and Susie away at the cottage, and Joey sleeping until noon, Carol got to spend the whole of Saturday morning doing what she loved to do; laying out projections, multi-year plans, and spreadsheets. It was so much more satisfying to work with figures and formulas. There were times when that realization gave her reason to pause and reconsider the life choices she had made—marriage, kids, and all that stuff—and there were times when she felt a little envious of people like C.C..

Still, Carol had never been the type of person who would go around feeling sorry for herself and once the kids had started school, she began taking online courses to keep herself current. She told Johnnie that it was for the business, but that was only partially true. She was also doing it to keep a part of herself alive—the part that had wanted to build and grow a business. Johnnie never really understood that but then again, he was a craftsman and not a business man.

Ben Davies was, and he was offering her the chance to do all of that. She still hadn't said no to him. He hadn't pushed her either. He said he could wait until the beginning of the new year for her answer. He had said that someone like her was worth waiting for.

She wished she had someone she could talk with about all of that, it was far too big a decision to make on her own. It was going to have an impact on all of them. But who? She had lost contact with most of her friends over the years. They had all started families of their own and despite the best of intentions, there was never enough time. Like herself and Johnnie, their whole lives had become dominated by their children.

Ben said that he had never experienced that. Between his daughter's illness, his strained marriage, and the fact that he hid in his office from all the problems that home had meant for him, he never went through any of that. Instead, he had been what he described as a man who spent far too long in a cocoon.

Sometimes, especially when Johnnie and Joey were going at it, Carol envied him. Except the part about losing his daughter, but even that had been turned into a positive. Ben was a very remarkable person, that way. But he was divorced.

Some of her friends had gone through divorce and it changed everything between them. Just like when she and Johnnie first got married and they only hung out with other married couples. And just like they had less and less in common with their single friends, her divorced friends no longer fitted in.

They had stayed in touch for the first few stages, being there and listening through the healing and the reforming. Offering support but trying to remain unbiased, particularly when she knew both sides of the story. But sooner or later they would drift apart—almost like being divorced was something that might be catching.

"Where is everybody?" Joey asked from the doorway. He had slept in his clothes and he had really bad bed-head.

"They went to the cottage; didn't they tell you?"

"I don't know; they might have."

Carol paused for a moment. Johnnie had behaved oddly when they were leaving, like there was something he wanted to say but didn't know how. Carol noticed, but didn't push it. They would talk about it when he was ready. In the meantime, she would deal with what was right in front of her.

"When we the last time you showered?"

"I don't know; a few days ago."

"Joey!"

"What?"

"Go up and shower right now."

"Why?"

"Because I want to take you out for brunch."

He tried to look disinterested, but he couldn't; he was always hungry. He couldn't just be compliant, either. He was stuck. "Now," Carol insisted. "And put on some clean clothes."

"Why?"

"Because I said so."

He tried to stare her down, but he was never going to win that battle. She could see inside of him, all the way down to the little boy who used to back himself into a corner and needed her help to get himself out.

"Now!"

He did and when he came back down, he looked a little sheepish. "Where we going?"

"Wherever you like."

He picked Nando's. It wouldn't have been her choice, but she went along with it. He was going through his 'hot spice' phase. He had gotten into a competition with his father over it until indigestion caught up with Johnnie and Carol had to intervene so he could save face.

"So?" Carol asked when he had finally pulled his chicken apart and, after spattering it with piri-piri, began to devour each piece. "What are we going to do with you?"

"Nothing."

"Joey, you know me too well to think that is going to work. You and I are going to sort this out right now, whether you like it or not."

"Is that why you are pretending to be nice to me?"

"Joey. I am your mother. I am genetically programmed to feed you. Don't read too much into it."

He hesitated for a moment. He never knew how to react when she spoke to him like that.

"I am also genetically programmed to tell you to wipe the grease off your face. Right now," she added sharply when he tried to shrug her off. He could be such an ass, sometimes, but she understood. He was a dichotomy. He was all that was Johnnie and her, rolled into one. And he was going through puberty.

He wiped his face, but he missed a spot. Without hesitation, she dipped her napkin in her water and cleaned it off.

"Mom! There are people watching."

"I know. That's why I used water. Would you prefer if I had used my spit instead?"

"That's gross."

"You think?" She stared him down. "Listen, Joey. Right now, I am your best chance at sorting this mess out. You want to work with me, or not?"

"What mess?"

"Joey!"

"It's no big deal, Mom. You guys were always telling me that I could do whatever I liked with my life and now that I do know, you are both having canaries."

It might have sounded like defiance, but Carol could hear something else. The small voice of a little boy who was lost. "Okay," she agreed. "But just so I have it straight, explain your plan to me again."

"Again?"

"Yes, again."

"I just want to quit school, Mom. I can't take it anymore."

There was something in his voice and that made her pause. He wasn't just whining; he was really trying to reach out to her, just as she had always taught him to do. And that just made everything so much more difficult.

When she was pregnant with him, she and Johnnie had talked about things like that—they used to talk about everything back then. Perhaps it was the well-intentioned naiveté of first-time parents, or it was a reaction to the strict, matter-of-fact way she had been raised. Regardless, they had agreed to always be honest and open with their children. They wanted to be the type of parents their kids could come to with their problems. And they would not be there as friends, but as wise and unemotional guides and yet not devoid of love and compassion. Super parents, as if such a thing was possible, but that had been their commitment. One they had promised to uphold, regardless.

"And, if we were to consider allowing you to do that, what is your plan?"

"I want to go and work with Dad."

"Okay, but what if your father doesn't want that? You can't force him to let you work with him."

"I know that, but you can."

Chapter 18

"So?" Mary asked when Gloria finally came down to the kitchen. She had agreed to stay in bed and rest after all of her exertions over the weekend. "Did you enjoy the kids' visit?"

"Wasn't it wonderful?" Gloria agreed and made her way to the window. "But it was a shame that Buddy wasn't with them. Was she not invited?"

"Oh, I'm sure she was, but she was probably busy. As you said, yourself, she has those two little hell-raisers."

"Did I say that? It doesn't sound like me. I love all of my great grandchildren, but I am concerned about Buddy. She is probably feeling very left-out. I wonder if somebody shouldn't call her?"

"If by somebody, do you mean me?"

"Not at all, Mary. You have more than enough to do, already." Gloria turned away from the window and began searching for something.

"Can I help you?" Mary asked.

"I am just looking for my glasses."

"They are on top of your head."

"And so they are, how forgetful of me. Now where did I leave the telephone?"

"Never mind; I'll call her."

"Call who?"

Mary waited while Gloria wandered off. She needed a few moments to find the right frame of mind.
She didn't want it to seem like she was meddling. She
had managed to piece together the snippets she had
gleaned from Johnnie, C.C., and Susie. Poor Buddy;
they really should have invited her too. She wasn't
blaming anybody; it was just an oversight. But it was
the type of thing that could set Buddy off and she had
more than enough on her plate.

*

"Is this a good time to talk?"

That caught Buddy on the hop. Usually, her mother would just start talking. "Sure. Mom. What's up?"

"I was just calling to see how you were. We missed
you over the weekend."

"Yeah. They asked me to come, but I was too busy
with the kids and all. How was it?"

"It was very nice, and Gloria really enjoyed herself. I think it was just what she needed, she has been
so distracted lately. And a bit morose."

"It's probably just the winter."

"I'm sure you're right, but I think we all have to
start facing up to the fact that Gloria is not getting
any younger, either."

Buddy knew what her mother was driving towards, but she wasn't going to make it easy for her.
And not for any selfish reason. If they were ever going
to have a healthy relationship, she was going to have
to break their old patterns. She was going to force her
mother to come out and actually say what was on her
mind. "None of us are getting any younger, Mom."

"Oh, don't be silly, dear. You are still young and healthy."

"For now." Buddy didn't mean to sound so pathetic; she just wanted her mother to show some concern for her.

"Buddy, I heard about the situation with Norm's job. Is there anything I can do?"

"You wouldn't happen to have a million dollars lying around?"

"If I had, it would be yours. But money is not always the best solution."

"I know, Mom, and I am sorry. I am just a bit worried about what will happen."

"Norm will find another job. You'll see."

"But what if it takes a while?"

'Buddy, we may not be the ideal family but we do look after each other when it really counts."

"We do?"

It was true, but Buddy wasn't willing to see that right now. She had been going through their budget and she couldn't see how they could make it all work. Sure, Norm would have his bonus. And he would be entitled to some type of severance package, but what would happen after that?

"Buddy. I know this may not be your top priority, but have you given any thought to Christmas?"

She had, and the whole idea filled her with dread. How could they possible spend money on Christmas knowing that the new year could be awful. "Not really."

"That's understandable, but I think you might want to consider a visit. For Gloria's sake, if for nothing else."

"I will think about it, Mom. Okay?"

"Do, please. It would mean the world to Gloria, and who knows how many more Christmases she has?"

Buddy was tempted to say that was how the last weekend of the summer happened, but she didn't. Instead she asked: "Did Johnnie say what he and Carol were doing?"

"He didn't, but I am sure they are coming. Why do you ask?"

"No reason." But that was not true. Buddy had to talk with Carol. After what she had said to Johnnie, she had to try to make things right before they all got together again.

"Hi, Carol. Is this a good time to talk?"

"That depends on what you want to talk about."

"Well . . . I . . . ah . . ."

"I was just kidding, Buddy. What's on your mind?"

"Oh. Well I was just talking to Mom."

"And let me guess; the issue of Christmas came up?"

"Well, yeah. Along with some other things. Have you and Johnnie talked about it—or any other stuff about the family?"

"Not really. We have had so many new and exciting challenges to deal with. I suppose you heard about Joey?"

"I did. Is there anything I can do to help? I haven't up to now because I didn't want to meddle." Buddy knew about C.C.'s visit to the school and wanted to register the point with Carol that she would never do anything like that. It was so typical of C.C. to jump in without even thinking about what she was saying. But then again, she had always been like that.

"Thanks, Buddy, but there's not much to do right now. It's between Johnnie and Joey and, with all due credit to your wonderful brother, he can be a bit of a mule sometimes. And his son is a chip off the old block."

"Are you and Johnnie doing okay?"

"Alright, I suppose. Why do you ask?"

"Oh, no reason. I would just think this is putting a bit of a strain on your relationship."

Carol laughed at that. "Johnnie and I don't have a relationship; we are married with kids."

"Yes, but you guys still love each other. Right?"

"Buddy, that is an odd thing to say—even for you."

"Oh, you know me, Carol"

"I do. So why don't you tell me what's really on your mind?"

"Well, as I am sure you know, Norm and I have been going through a bit of a tough time, too. His company is closing down and that has made things difficult between us. And everything had been going so well up until then."

"Yeah, Johnnie mentioned it a few times. I don't think you should be too worried. Norm will find something else; it just might take some time."

"I realize that—now. At first, I went a bit crazy and started thinking that the problem was me. He didn't want to tell me and I started to imagine things like he didn't love me anymore, or that he had fallen in love with someone else, or something crazy like that. Does that ever happen to you?"

"If only we could be so lucky, eh, Bud?"

"No. I am being serious."

"Buddy. We have all known Norm for a while now and while he may have his peculiarities, it is obvious how much he still loves you."

"And Johnnie still loves you."

"He does? Since when?"

"I'm serious, Carol."

"I know, Buddy, and I know the big lug is still crazy about me."

"But are you still crazy about him?"

"Buddy? What are you driving at?"

"Oh, nothing. I guess I have just been thinking about Christmas, and all, and I just want it to be perfect for everybody."

"Did your mother put you up to this?"

"Not really. She was just telling me that Gloria isn't doing so well and it got me thinking, but I am sure Johnnie mentioned it to you."

"He didn't, but Susie did."

"What did she say?"

"That your mother and Gloria are hatching a plot to get us all together for Christmas—only not in those exact words."

"So? Will you and Johnnie think about it? After all we really should make an effort for Gloria's sake. This is her first Christmas since Jake died."

Carol said nothing to that and Buddy knew she had hit a nerve. "I mean, it must have been hard enough to have her son die, but to have to watch while he paddled out . . . That's not something a mother should ever have to do. It kind of makes all of our problems seem far less important."

"Okay, okay, Buddy. Johnnie and I will talk about it and get back to you."

"Thanks, Carol, I knew I could count on you."

"That's me. Good old reliable Carol."

"I always thought so."

"You're so sweet. But let me ask you something. What else is on your mind?"

"Nothing, why do you ask?"

"No reason. Besides, I am sure I will find out sooner or later."

*

After she hung up, Carol thought about it for a little while. Buddy was up to something—other than the obvious. There was something she had wanted to say but couldn't. It could be anything, so Carol decided to file it away for now. In the meantime, she had to set her own wheels in motion. She had thought it all through and she was ready to talk to someone about it. She picked up her phone before she could second-guess herself. "C.C.? Would you have time for lunch?"

C.C. had suggested Scaramouche; she was almost insistent on it.

"God, I haven't been here in years," she announced when they were seated.

"I was here a few weeks ago," Carol mentioned casually as she briefly scanned the menu. "The pasta is still great."

"Really?" C.C. answered from behind her menu. "I didn't think that Johnnie did places like this."

"Actually, I was here with a client."

"You really know how to wine and dine them."

"It was his treat."

"Nice; do tell me more."

"Well, his name is Ben Davis and he made a proposal that I think I am about to accept."

"Oh, really?"

"Yes. He is planning to buy up old cinemas and restore them as multipurpose venues. You know screenings, live shows and things like that. And, he has invited me to partner with him."

"As a business partner. Right?"

"No. I was planning on starting my cabaret career—and maybe do a few movies on the side. Of course, as a business partner. What the hell else would it be?"

"Does Johnnie know about this?"

"I haven't told him yet."

"And should I ask why?"

"Because I can't work for him and do this at the same time. And with the way things have been going for him, he might see it as the rat leaving the sinking ship."

"Are things that bad?"

"They are heading there, but that is another thing about this project. It could keep Johnnie in work for the next few years. He could even take on Joey and kill two birds."

"So why not tell him?"

"Because I need to figure out the financing. Ben has enough money to get started, but I don't want to go in with that understanding. I want it to be an equal partnership. And I don't want to take on investors if we don't have to."

"How much would you need?"

"About three million. That, along with Ben's money, would be enough to finance most of the first project. After that, we would have to borrow against the existing properties we already own. But interest rates are still not too bad"

"Where would you get that kind of money?"

"That's the problem, C.C.. Even if we remortgaged the house, it still wouldn't be enough. Not that Johnnie would ever go for that. As far as he was concerned, we couldn't pay our original mortgage off fast enough."

"So, you need to convince your husband to help you raise money while telling him that you will not be running his business anymore. Am I missing anything?"

"That's pretty much it in a nutshell."

They ate in silence for a while, each lost in their own thoughts, until C.C. looked up from her plate and smiled. "Buddy could work for Johnnie. You could show her the ropes and then still be around if she messes up."

"And I thought your solution to Joey's problem was bad."

"You are never going to let me live that down. Are you?"

"C.C., I have the world of respect for you and all you have accomplished in your professional life. And I am always holding you up as a role model for Susie, but your personal life . . . Kiddo, you are a walking disaster."

"And all this time I thought you just saw me as a pain in the ass. Anyway, that is a bunch of news. Leave it with me and I will see if there is anything I can do—professionally.

"By the way," C.C. added with a grin. Have you talked with Buddy recently?"

"As a matter of fact, I talked with her this morning. It was a little odd. I kept feeling she was trying to tell me something, but couldn't just come out and say it."

"That's our Buddy. Did she mention Christmas?"

"What do you think?"

Chapter 19

Norm had stayed late again, sitting in the office pretending that all was well. Some of the others were beginning to sense something was wrong but when they asked him, he denied any knowledge of it. "They need us," he would say in his most reassuring voice. "They couldn't run the place with us."

He felt bad about having to do that, but it was happening and there was nothing he could do about it—except look out for himself. A good 'transition' bonus would be enough to cover another three to four months. Plus, he would get a decent severance. All in all, he could make it last for up to twelve months if he had too.

When he had finally told Buddy, she had taken it better than he expected. The night she cooked him a steak, they had sat and talked it through. She'd seemed calm and, in a funny way, almost relieved. She'd said that she wasn't so concerned—now that she knew what the problem was—and that she had every confidence that he would find something in the new year. But he wasn't so sure. Everyone he had talked with said the same thing. Budgets and staffing had been set for now, and blah, blah, blah.

He kept telling himself that it would only be a matter of time, but he was getting a bad feeling deep in his guts. He felt like the earth was about to give way under his feet and when it did, he would be in freefall. He had to keep pushing that thought aside.

When he finally got home, he turned off the ignition and sat staring at his house. It was a modest, semi-detached three-bedroom and it was all he had to show for all of the years that he had been working his ass off. Before, when life had given him reasons to doubt, he would remind himself that it was the reason for getting back up every time he had been knocked down. It wasn't much but it was something. It was the payoff for getting up and going to work every day, whether he felt like it or not. In his more fanciful moments, he would look at it as a monument to all the little guys like him who took all the crap life could throw at them and kept on going. But, as the feeling in his guts kept reminding him, it wasn't really his. The bank still owned half of it and, if he had to sell it, the equity would hardly be enough to buy into anything that wasn't out in the back of the boonies.

It had all been a game and it was about to come to an end. He had been juggling too many balls while walking on a tight rope and now someone had shaken him off. It was all very well for Jack to say it wasn't personal, but how much more personal could it get?

If it was just him, he might have shrugged it off and started all over again—he'd had to do that a few times before. But it wasn't just him anymore; he was a father and a husband now. The last ten years had been all about his commitment to his family. A commitment he might not be able to keep anymore.

That was when the feeling in his guts would surge up and he wanted to run. Sometimes, he even thought about it. He could start the car and go somewhere. He could go to a bar and get shit-faced. Hell, he could even drive to the airport and fly off somewhere. There was still room on the credit cards. He could use that before Buddy got to it.

That was the hardest part of it all. He and Buddy had never really been partners. She always said they were, but that hadn't been his experience. Usually, when the shit hit the fan, she was the first one to turn on him. No matter what happened, everything had to be about her and the way she was feeling—and all of her other issues. She would say it was all about the kids, and stuff like that, but it always ended up the same way. Even when they did talk about their problems, he never got to tell her what he was going through.

When he told her he was losing his job, it was the same. Somehow, she quickly managed to make it all about everything else. She was concerned about what it would do to the kids—having to move and change schools and all that stuff—and instead of being able to talk about himself he had spent the rest of the evening trying to reassure her.

Sometimes, he wondered what it would be like to walk away and start again with somebody new— somebody who wasn't so self-obsessed all the time. Somebody who could actually see him for what he really was and not just as a second-rate husband and father.

He had to face up to it, his life was crap but he really only had himself to blame. When he and Buddy first got together, all he ever wanted was to be there for her. He wanted to be the guy she could smile with when all the shit with her family got her down.

He had tried to live up to his end of the deal and what did it get him? He had gotten walked all over. Buddy would say that it wasn't her, that it was the way life had made her, but at the end of the day it really didn't matter. Whatever crap life threw at her would end up being thrown at him, sooner or later.

After he had vented his frustrations, that day at the cottage, he had settled down and really tried to make things right between them. And when her father killed himself, he had done everything he could. He told her that he got what she was going through and that he would be there for her. He told her that he would be more patient and that all the things that had happened before would be forgotten. But it was all just bullshit. Well-meaning and all that, but it was still bullshit. How could anybody be expected to let all of that slide? It was what they were together. It was what their lives had really been about.

It was all very well for her to say that she was going to change. And it was all very well for him to say that he was going to be loving and supportive, but what was he supposed to do with all the crap that had built up inside of him? All the years that she dumped her emotional garbage all over him and everything he had ever tried to do for her. What was he supposed to do with that?

And it wasn't like he hadn't tried. He had tried to become all the things he said he would be; a good father, a good husband, and a good provider. But now, all of that was being taken out of his hands.

And even that would become all about her, too. He could see it already. Sure, he should have told her earlier, but he knew how she would have reacted. Buddy wasn't the type of partner that you could share real problems with.

He might have sat in the car all night, but it was getting cold. And his family were waiting.

*

Carol sat on the bed and applied her hand cream. It was the last part of her nightly ritual that often took as much as twenty minutes. Johnnie, in the meantime, had brushed his teeth, put on his sleeping tee-shirt and his pajamas and had already rolled over.

"I had lunch with your sister, today."

"That's nice. Which one?" He answered without looking at her.

"C.C.."

"Oh, and should I ask what you two are up to?"

"Just because I had lunch with your sister doesn't mean that I am up to something."

He rolled over and looked at her. "Then why are you telling me?"

It had been another strained evening when they all had dinner and did whatever they were doing with as little contact as possible. An uneasy truce had settled and no one wanted to say, or do, whatever it was that might cause things to erupt again. Carol didn't mind too much. Sometimes in families, things had to be that way but right now, she needed the two of them to be on the same page—or at least agree on which page that was. "Because you and I need to talk about something."

"Can't it wait?"

"Until when? Until you get up and run out of the house in the morning? You can't go on avoiding us."

"I am not avoiding anything. I just figured that the less I am around, the less chance of things with Joey . . . you know."

"Just Joey?"

"What's that supposed to mean?"

"It means that I feel you have been avoiding me too."

"Oh Carol. Let it go. You are beginning to sound like one of my sisters."

"Which one?"

That almost brought a smile so he rolled over again. She reached out and touched his shoulder. He stiffened a little, so she drew back.

"Johnnie. Do you remember me mentioning Ben Davis?"

"The guy with the cinema project? Don't tell me; we were underbid on that one too."

"No, in fact, we got that job, but there is a whole lot more to it."

"Like?"

"Well, first of all, The Royale is just the beginning."

She laid it all out for him; all the possibilities and all of the projections. She had been tempted to get her laptop and show him all the graphs and charts she had prepared. He did get excited and she knew that in his mind, he was already hard at work, tearing down and restoring. Until she mentioned the partnership idea.

"How would that work? First, we don't have the money, and second, we don't have the money."

"Let me worry about that part. Now, assuming we could pull it all together, are you going to be okay with me working on it? Working full-time on it?"

He sat up and reached out to her. He drew her close and let her rest her head on his chest where she could feel his heart beat. "If it is what you want to do, then I will be okay with it."

"You realize that we won't be able to go on working the way we did?"

"Yeah. That will be a problem, but we can figure something out."

"I think I already have."

"Not Buddy?"

"No, even though C.C. thought it might be a good idea."

"C.C. thought that giving Joey's school a hard time was a good idea."

"I was thinking of Norm."

"You're kidding?"

"Not really. He's a good logistics guy, and he can deal with people."

"Since when?"

"Oh, be nice. I think he could handle it and I will be there to keep him from screwing up—at least for the first few months."

"I don't know. Working with Norm . . . Let me think about it."

"Sure. There's no point in talking to him until we figure out the money side of things."

"We?"

"Yes, unless working with your wife has gotten to be too much for you."

"Been doing it for years. What's a few more?"

"As partners; from now on I will be a client. Your biggest and most important client."

"Boss, client, wife, it's pretty much the same thing."

"Glad you figured that part out."

"So? You and this Ben guy; what's the story there?"

"Oh, you know; the usual. He met me, fell hopelessly in love with me, and now wants to spend every minute of the day with me. Does that worry you?"

"Not really."

"Not even a little?"

"No. After a few months of him, you'll come crawling back, begging me to give you another chance."

"And will you?"

"Depends."

"Careful there, big boy. There's lots of cheaper contractors out there."

"I'm not worried. You've had the best. How could you possibly settle for less?"

She nestled closer to him and began to nuzzle his neck while her hand began to roam across his chest. "I am so glad you will consider it and it could mean that you could take Joey on as an apprentice."

*

"I was wondering how long you were going to sit out there," Buddy remarked when Norm finally made his way to their bedroom. She had been watching something on her tablet as she sat up waiting for him.

"What do you mean?" He asked and sat on the bed with his back to her. He didn't want her to see his face. He just wanted to get into bed, pull the covers over his head, and be done with another day.

"I saw you, sitting outside in the car."

"Oh, that. I was just thinking about stuff, you know. Clearing my mind so I don't bring it all home with me." He took off his shirt and pants and piled them on the chair. Normally Buddy would complain about that, but he didn't care.

This time, she didn't. She just put away her tablet so she could focus all of her attention on him.

"Norm. Can I ask you something? Are you ever afraid of telling me about your problems?"

"I am telling you. It's just the shit from the office. I hate that I have to pretend that everything is normal. I just think the rest of the guys should know."

"Is that all that is bothering you?"

"Pretty much. I worked with some of these guys for a few years. I think they deserve to be treated better." He turned briefly and tried to smile. Then he lay down with his back to her and pulled the covers up to his face.

"Norm, you know you can share your feelings with me. I know you are probably worried about how I might react, but I am reacting anyway. I know I start thinking of all kinds of crazy things, but I want to be there for you."

"Thanks, but right now I really just need to get some sleep."

"Okay, but just remember that there are people who are rooting for you."

"Who else knows?"

"Just my family, and they all want to help any way the can."

Norm didn't answer. That was the last thing he needed to hear. None of her family, other than Johnnie, had ever taken him seriously and now he would be the guy that needed their help to look after his own family.

"And speaking of family," Buddy continued. "We need to talk about what we are going to do about Christmas. I didn't tell you before, but Dwayne said something that made me stop and think."

Norm listened to what his son had said and it made him stop and think, too. Everything he had done, and everything he had striven for, was measured by one thing. It wasn't just about him and Buddy; it was about his children. And they would have a Christmas they would remember, even if it cost him more than he had. It was the whole point of family.

"So? What do you want to do?"

"I would prefer a nice, quiet Christmas at home— you know, just the four of us."

"We can do that."

"But I think there are plans to do it at the cottage. How would you feel about that?"

"Let's do both."

"Oh, Norm. Be realistic."

"Why?" he laughed and pushed aside everything that had been weighing on him. He was a father, and a husband. They were parts of him that meant more than how much he earned. "After all," he rolled over and took Buddy in his arms. "Christmas only comes once a year."

Chapter 20

C.C. had been most persistent, Carol and Buddy had to free up some time and join her for brunch. She had texted both of them to say there were a few very pressing matters that she needed to talk with them about, and she was waiting for them when they arrived. She had also insisted on going to Lady Marmalade on Queen Street and they had agreed because neither of them had ever been.

"So?" Carol asked after they had been seated and served their lattes. "What are you up to, now?"

"Ladies," C.C. began like she was addressing a committee meeting. "I have been giving a great deal of thought to the dilapidated state of our family and have decided that it has now fallen to the three of us to come together and start to put things right."

Both Carol and Buddy groaned, but C.C. ignored them.

"We are," she continued like she was working from a rehearsed script, "going through, what Shakespeare once called, 'the winter of our discontent.'"

"Oh, dear," Carol muttered as an aside to Buddy.

"Please," C.C. admonished both of them. "Hear me out and then I will be more than happy to field your questions, comments, and any other observations you may have, whether they are relevant or not."

"Really, C.C.?"

"Yes, really, Carol. What we have here is what could be referred to as a 'family in crisis.'" She even made the quotation marks with her fingers. "Our grandmother is failing, our mother has gone into hiding, both your husbands are getting lost in some kind or existential crisis, and your," she pointed at Carol, "children have been left to wander in the wastelands of adolescence. Now, I don't mean to offend anyone, but this is the way I see it."

Buddy looked a bit confused and Carol looked bemused, so C.C. continued. She had decided to play it over the top. "Have I missed anything?"

"Yes," Carol answered, clearly getting into the spirit. "Having analyzed and evaluated our lives with such clarity, I am wondering why you haven't told us anything about your own situation."

"Ah, that. Well, if you must know, Heather and I are taking a break from each other."

"Oh?"

"Yes. We talked and decided that we were not in the same place in the relationship and that, for now, we should step back and reevaluate."

She tried to make it sound as practical and as matter-of-fact as she could because it was still fresh and raw. She and Heather had talked a couple of nights before and C.C. had put it out there. It was part of her new approach; she would challenge her greatest fears, directly. She felt that Heather was stringing her along and it was time to call her on it.

She hadn't expected Heather to agree with her and, afterwards, she had cried herself to sleep like a love-sick teenager, but it felt better by the morning. At least it was out there now.

"I am sorry to hear that," Carol offered and reached out to touch C.C.'s hand.

"And I am sorry, too," Buddy added and put her hand on Carol's.

"Well then," C.C. blinked back a tear and put her other hand on top of Buddy's. "Let's make a pact. Let's start putting this whole mess right. Who is with me?"

They had to move their hands because their food arrived and it spoiled the effect C.C. had been going for. They had all ordered something different so they could share. Buddy had picked the Eggs Benedict, Carol had opted for the Crepe Croque Monsieur, and C.C. had gone with the Moroccan Scramble. She needed something to make the morning feel a little more exotic.

"Are you going to be okay?" Buddy asked after they had all tasted their food, and each other's.

"Oh, you know me, Sis. I will bounce back from this. I always do."

"Yes," Buddy agreed. "You always do. But will you be okay—inside?"

"Of course, she will," Carol answered before C.C. had to react. "She just needs some new and wonderful adventure to keep her busy in the meantime. I suppose," she turned to C.C., "that's what this is really about?"

"Carol," C.C. replied as she put aside her 'girly' feelings and got back to her plan. "You might be right. I do have a poor track record when it comes to things like this. But I am changing that. This time, instead of rushing out to find someone to take Heather's place, I am going to use all of my energies to try to make

213

things better for those who have always loved me, and stood with me all along."

"Oh, that's so sweet," Buddy said in her mothering voice. "And I know what you mean about trying to change."

"Yes, it is sweet," Carol agreed as she eyed C.C. with some misgivings. "So, what's the plan?"

"Well," C.C. answered in a more controlled voice. "I think the three of us need to put our heads together and start to sort out a few things. And the first thing we need to agree on is: Are we going to get everyone together at the cottage for Christmas?"

"I'm not sure that Norm and I are in the mood for a family Christmas this year. We might end up doing something quiet at home."

"I see," C.C. nodded and turned to Carol. "And you?"

"Well, I was thinking of running off to the Algarve with my fancy man."

C.C. smiled at that, but Buddy just squirmed a little. "Oh, you heard about that."

"Of course, I heard. Nothing in this family stays secret for very long."

"I'm sorry. I didn't mean anything by it."

"Don't worry about it, Buddy. Johnnie and I talked and we are fine with it. Besides, it was very flattering, in a way."

"But you'd never do anything like that to Johnnie, would you?"

"Let it go Buddy."

"Ladies," C.C. interjected. "We digress. Here's what I think we need to agree on: That we are all going to go to the cottage and make this the best Christmas ever. Who's with me?"

*

Since his night in the car, Norm had bounced back. Life, he had decided, was what it was and there was no point in dwelling on that. Instead, he would pick himself up, dust himself off, and start all over again. He didn't know any other way of dealing with things.

"So, I guess you've heard the wonderful news," he joked as he poured out the first beers. He and Johnnie were having another boys' night out. Buddy had suggested it and this time; they had decided to go to Scruffy Murphy's on Eglinton.

"About Christmas? That's the last thing I need right now."

"Ah, c'mon. It won't be that bad and the kids will love it."

"Maybe your kids will. My kids are at that age when stuff like this doesn't mean anything anymore."

"You know Johnnie. I have always thought the best of you. I always thought that you were a solid guy. I'd even go as far as saying that I have always looked up to you, but I can't say any of that anymore."

"Really? And why is that?"

"Because you are turning into one big fun-sucker."

"Thanks. That's what I was going for."

"Well, in that case, you rule."

"Is this going to be one of those nights?"

"If you mean that my wife sent me here to persuade you, then yes."

"Yeah, Carol made me come, too."

"So why don't we do what good husbands do."

"And what would that be?"

"We just put our tails between our legs and just go along with it all. Then, when we are up there, we can sneak off and do some ice-fishing. We can drag the shed out on the ice and spend the whole night drinking beer and no one will come bothering us."

"We'll freeze our balls off."

"You know, you are not just a fun-sucker, you are becoming a wussy boy, too. The Johnnie that I knew would have jumped at a chance like that."

"You are not going to let this go, are you?"

"Sorry, man. I would if I could."

"Because of Buddy?"

"Yup, and C.C. and Carol, too. They had a meeting."

"Yeah, I heard."

"So, let's do it?"

"Can you give me one good reason why I should do it—other than doing what the sisterhood demands?"

"And isn't that reason enough? But let me give you another. In the words of the great and wise Don Vito Corleone: 'A man who doesn't spend time with his family can never be a real man.'"

"Really, Norm? You're going to quote family values from a mobster?"

"There are things that have to be done and you do them and you never talk about them. You don't try to justify them. They can't be justified. You just do them. Then you forget it."

"The Don didn't say that."

"No, but Michael did. And here's something else to think about: 'You cannot say no to the people you love, not often. That's the secret. And then when you do, it has to sound like a yes. Or you have to make them say no. You have to take time and trouble.'"

"Did you memorize the whole book?"

"No. I just watched the movies the other night. I thought it would help me figure out how I am going to handle the rest of my wonderful life."

"And what have you figured out?"

"That the real winners in life are the guys who get up once more than they are knocked down."

"Did I ever tell you the story of Billy Banged-up?"

"Was he in The Godfather?"

"No, he was one of the kids who grew up near the cottage. We used to play shinny together when the lake was frozen."

"Doesn't sound as exciting as The Godfather, but go ahead."

"Well, one day we were all there—about ten of us. One of the kids was this big, bruiser who kept knocking Billy over. Billy was like a rat on the ice. He was one of those guys that carried his stick high."

"Like Kenny Linseman?"

"Yeah, except this kid had no talent. Anyway, he got into it with the big guy and they dropped the gloves. It didn't last long. The big guy decked him, but Billy didn't stay down. He got back up and the big guy decked him again, knocking out one of his front teeth.

"It was weird," Johnnie added as he stared into his glass. "All the others guys just stood around and watched.

"Billy got up again and got knocked down again. It happened a few more times and the big guy didn't want any more part of it. He asked the rest of us to jump in and pull Billy away, but nobody did. We all just stood around watching.

"Then it got really ugly. Billy kept getting up and the big guy kept knocking him down. Both of his front teeth were gone and his face was a bloody mess.

"And the worst part was, we all just stood around watching. Nobody even tried to stop it."

"That's a sad story. What was the point you were trying to make?"

"It means that I will do it."

*

The following morning, Buddy called Mary to tell her the news. C.C. and Carol had felt that it would be better coming from her.

Mary was delighted, but she was also concerned that it was a lot of upheaval. "Are you sure, Rosebud? I wouldn't want everybody to have to go to so much trouble."

"It's no trouble, Mom, unless you and Gloria wouldn't be happy about it?"

"Of course not. Gloria and I would be delighted, but will it be safe? The roads up here can be treacherous this time of the year."

"We'll be fine, Mom."

"Okay, but please tell Johnnie and Norm to be careful and not to go racing, or anything like that."

"I will, Mom, and don't worry. They are both very responsible, especially when it comes to family."

"I am so glad to hear you say that, Rosebud."

Buddy knew exactly what her mother meant by that and, after she had hung up, she sat in the warm glow of it all. It had been a struggle, but it was all coming together so nicely. It might be the best Christmas they had so far.

*

Gloria was sitting by the kitchen window, staring out towards the island. Mary had given up trying to deflect her from it; there was no point. Gloria was fading; there could be no doubt about it.

"That was Buddy on the phone."

"How nice, and is she keeping well?"

"She sounds well and she called to tell me that they have all talked and they are coming for Christmas. Isn't that good news?"

It took Gloria a moment to react. She slowly turned from the window and fixed her gaze on Mary. "I am very happy for you."

"You should be happy for yourself, too. The whole family will be here and we will have a wonderful Christmas."

"I am glad," Gloria agreed, but it seemed so empty. "I am very glad," she repeated and turned back to the window.

"Gloria? What is the matter?"

"It is nothing, dear. I am just feeling a little worn out, but I am sure I will be much better when they are here."

"Yes, and I don't want you to worry about anything. Buddy and C.C. are going to come up early and help me get everything ready before the others arrive."

"Buddy and C.C.?"

"Yes. It seems like those two are becoming the best of friends these days."

"That's nice."

Mary let it go at that. For the last few days, Gloria seemed to be having difficulty keeping her thoughts together. She would often just drift away in the middle of a sentence. Mary was concerned enough to call the doctor, but he didn't think it was so unusual—not for someone Gloria's age; given all that she had been through.

So, Mary left her in peace and went off to begin her lists. There was so much to do.

Chapter 21

"Dashing through the snow," C.C. sang as she steered against the skid. "In a one-horse open sleigh."

She had taken the turn in the road too fast and beneath the drifting snow, the surface was slippery. She had rented a practical SUV with four-wheel drive and wanted to see what it could do. She had told Johnnie and Buddy that she wouldn't be caught dead in it in the city, but it was perfect for the north country. She got to sit higher, and that gave her a very different perspective. She had also joked that it almost made her feel invincible. "In a one-horse open sleigh."

"C.C.!" Buddy pleaded from the back seat where she struggled to keep the bags of groceries from spilling onto the floor. "For God's sake, slow down."

"O'er the fields we go, laughing all the way," C.C. continued, but she did lighten up on the gas.

"What's the hurry?" Johnnie asked from the seat beside her. He was a nervous passenger at the best of times. He had offered to drive, but C.C. had insisted.

"I can't wait to get to Grandma's house and get this Christmas started."

"Since when did you become a fan of Christmas?"

"Yeah," Buddy chimed in. "Since when?"

"Since we decided to have it at the cottage," C.C. answered without looking at either of them. "Don't you guys remember what it was like when we were kids? Why the hell did we ever stop doing it there."

"You were the one who stopped coming," Buddy muttered as she repositioned herself among the piles of bags. They had done enough shopping to last the year. "After you went away to college and didn't want to have anything to do with the rest of us."

"Really?" C.C. adjusted the rearview mirror so she could look her sister in the eye. "Is that how you remember it?"

"Tell her, Johnnie," Buddy replied and reached forward to nudge her brother's shoulder.

"Yeah, Johnnie?" C.C. piled on. "Tell us what really happened."

"Kids!"

"What do you mean?"

"We started having kids and no one wanted the hassle of driving up here."

"I don't think that was the reason and it certainly wasn't why Norm and I stopped coming. The way I remember it was that Gloria stopped doing it."

"And that was because Mom made a big deal of it so Gloria started coming to the city instead."

"See!" C.C. added when Johnnie finished. "It had nothing to do with me."

"Well, I don't remember it that way," Buddy continued after thinking about it for a while. "I remember Gloria saying that it wasn't worth all the hassle if certain people weren't even going to make the effort."

"What's that supposed to mean?" C.C. turned around to face her sister and Johnnie had to grab the steering wheel while she did.

"It doesn't mean anything; it's just the way things were."

"Or just the way you have chosen to remember them."

"And what's that supposed to mean?"

Johnnie kept the car steady, but said nothing. His sisters had been bickering on and off since they had set out and it had almost erupted into open warfare when they stopped to do the shopping. They had agreed to split the bill three ways, but while Buddy had wanted to practice some restraint, C.C. had wanted to splurge. They had picked up two turkeys so that Johnnie and the boys could each have a drumstick, and a ham for Norm who didn't care for turkey; ingredients for three different stuffings because Gloria, Mary, and Buddy, all had their own recipes. They had also bought squash, sprouts, carrots, potatoes and cranberries—fresh in the bag as well as canned. Johnnie knew better than to get involved and had let it all go without comment. Instead, he had dutifully followed after them, pushing the shopping cart up and down each aisle as they bought more and more.

Buddy had her lists and stopped to compare prices and quantities. Then, when she had made her decision, she would carefully place each item in the cart. C.C. had a different approach and just grabbed whatever caught her eye and tossed it in on top of Buddy's neat organization. Johnnie had to smile at that.

"Who put the potatoes on top of the eggs?" Buddy had asked him and he just shrugged and got a second cart. But C.C. was going out of her way to be a pest and randomly piled her stuff in both.

He made no comment on that either and just hauled the carts along. He had known what he was getting himself into and had decided he would make the best of it.

Carol had insisted that he travel with his sisters and she would follow later with their kids. She felt that he should spend time with them and get through whatever they had to go through before the others got there. It had seemed like a wise idea at the time.

*

"T'is the season to be jolly," he sang loudly to interrupt them.

"Or it would be if certain people . . ." Buddy tried again from the back seat.

"Fa la la la la, la la la la," C.C. sang to drown her out.

"Maybe this is why we stopped doing Christmas at the cottage," he laughed and turned to look at each of his sisters.

It wasn't. There had been so many reasons. He and Carol had decided to have Joey's first Christmas at their place and his mother had been more than happy to go along with that. Then Susie came along and the pattern was set. And when Buddy and Norm started their family, it just made sense to stay in the city and alternate between their houses. If Gloria had any objections, she kept them to herself. But Johnnie always had the feeling that she was saddened by that. As time went by, he missed those Christmases at the cottage. Or maybe he missed who he had been back then.

"Well, I am glad we decided to come back," Buddy decided after staring out the window for a few moments. The trees along the roadside were covered with fresh, fluffy snow and the setting sun had a pinkish hue.

"We?" C.C. asked.

"Yes, we." Johnnie joined in. "Just because you decided to tag along, doesn't make it your idea."

223

"Oh, really."

"Do you remember the lights?" Buddy asked him, pointedly ignoring her sister. "I wonder if Gloria still has them. They were the old colored kind that looked so much better."

"Until one of them went out and the whole string had to be checked."

"But that was part of the fun. And the tree . . . do you remember going out to get the tree?"

"I don't remember that as fun. We could never agree on which tree."

"We?" Buddy asked and nodded her head in C.C.'s direction. "I think you mean certain people who shall remain nameless."

"That's because you always picked out crooked little scraggly things."

"I did not. Johnnie tell her."

He didn't. He just smiled. Despite everything, they were good times and as soon as the others got there, he would organize them all and go out into the woods and pick out the perfect tree. Joey and Susie had never done that as they had gotten their Christmas trees from the lot for years. Norm would be up for it too, and the little kids. It was going to be a blast.

"What are you smiling at," C.C. asked after she glanced over at him.

"Nothing."

"Oh, really. I know that smile. You are plotting something."

"Maybe," Buddy suggested and leaned forward into the space between the front seats. "He is just getting into the Christmas Spirit."

"Who him? More likely he's turning into the Grinch."

"Don we now our gay apparel," he sang and his sisters joined in and sang the la la las. Despite their banter, they were clearly enjoying being together again. Together without their spouses or children; like they had been so many years ago.

"I have decided," he announced when they finished singing. "That I am going to celebrate this Christmas like it was my last."

"Oh, don't say that. It sounds so ominous. You make it seem like . . ."

"Let him say what he wants," C.C. interrupted and looked over at Johnnie. "And what brought this about?"

"I have been doing a lot of thinking and I have decided that if I am stuck with this dysfunctional circus of a family, that I may as well enjoy it."

"That's the spirit."

"Do you really think we are dysfunctional?" Buddy asked and sounded a little concerned. "I certainly don't. I think we are as normal, and as well-adjusted, as anyone."

"Excuse me? But isn't that what dysfunctionality is all about?" C.C. laughed and powered through another bend in the road. "Being conditioned to normalize dysfunction and pretend it is okay. Face it; we are a bunch of screw-ups and have been since before we were born."

Johnnie said nothing to that. He just sat there and smiled. Whenever Buddy and C.C. got together it was like they were little kids again; always competing and poking each other. Sometimes, it got to him. And it would again, but right now he decided to let it pass. At least until after Christmas.

"That might be true in your case," Buddy piped up after a few moments of silence. She always had to stop and pick her words carefully when she got into it with her sister. "But some of us work hard to maintain our sanity."

"And some of us don't have to work so hard."

"If you mean that some of us are happier being crazy, then I have to agree with you."

"As the great Ralph Waldo Emerson said: To be yourself in a world that is constantly trying to make you something else is the greatest accomplishment."

"Yeah, yeah, yeah. You went to college. We all get that."

"Don't blame me because you made different choices."

"I am very happy with the choices I made."

"Really?"

"What is that supposed to mean?"

"Kids," Johnnie interrupted. "It is all about the kids."

"What is?"

"Christmas. I knew that when Joey and Susie were younger. I guess I forgot it as they grew up."

Buddy and C.C. stopped their bickering and both looked at him. "Do go on," C.C. encouraged.

"We get so caught up in all the crap life throws at us and we forget what it was like when we were kids and Christmas was the time when magic could still happen."

"What have you been smoking?" C.C. laughed again.

"Don't be like that," Buddy chided. "Let him share his feelings."

"That is why, when we get there, we are going to celebrate like it is the last Christmas the world will ever know."

"Well, Norm and I will do everything we can to make that happen."

"Norm and you? Have you merged into one person?"

"And that," Johnnie continued before Buddy had time to respond, "is why both of you are going to behave like adults and let the kids enjoy themselves."

"I am not the one who is behaving like a child."

"Are so."

"Am not. Johnnie. Tell her I am not."

"Yeah. Run to Johnnie. Go and hide behind your big brother."

"Oh, yeah. Well . . ."

"It's beginning to look a lot like Christmas everywhere you go," Johnnie sang and tapped his fingers in time.

"Or it would be if it weren't for certain people who shall remain nameless."

"What time is Norm going to get here?" He asked to distract Buddy as C.C. accelerated into another turn.

"He is coming tomorrow afternoon with the kids. They have school and he is having a farewell lunch with the people he worked with. Why?"

"Just asking."

"Is Carol coming tomorrow, too?"

"If her trip to the Algarve falls through."

"Oh. You know about that."

"Everyone knows about that," C.C. piped up. "I made a point of telling them."

"I'm sorry about that," Buddy offered, ignoring her sister. "I didn't mean anything by it. You know the way I get some times."

"Like when you are off your meds?"

"C.C.," Johnnie chided and turned to face Buddy. "Forget it, Sis. Carol saw the funny side of it."

"That's good, but if you really want me to forget about it; why do you keep bringing it up?"

"Yeah, Johnnie," C.C. asked in mock earnest. "Why do you keep bringing it up? We all know that Buddy has her issues. Why do you keep having to rub her nose in them?"

"Yeah, Johnnie." Buddy joined in from the back seat. It was just like old times. The two of them would fight like cats and dogs until someone tried to step between them.

"I'll be home for Christmas," he sang in response. "If only in my dreams."

"Wow. You really got this dark, broody Christmas thing going. Lighten up already."

He laughed and looked over at C.C.. "I have missed this."

"What?"

"Just the three of us spending time together."

"Ah, that's so sweet of you to say." Buddy reached forward and caressed his arm.

"Don't buy it, Sis," C.C. cautioned. "He always says one thing and means another."

"You're right," Johnnie agreed. "A few hours with the two of you has confirmed everything Carol has been telling me."

"Oh? And what is that?"

"That she and I should move to the Algarve."

"And what about your kids?"

"They are going to move in with their Aunt C.C.. Apparently, she has become an expert on how the next generation should be raised."

Chapter 22

The farewell lunch had been awkward and Norm had to bite his tongue so many times. Especially when Jack got up and told everybody how difficult a decision it had been. He made it seem like he had fought every step of the way but in the end, it was something that had been decided above his head. He was losing his job, too. He made a point of mentioning that, several times, but what he didn't mention was his payoff. Rumors from Payroll put it as high as three years' salary—not bad for a guy who already had something else lined up. It might have gotten to Norm, but he kept reminding himself of something C.C. had said to him.

She had called to talk to him about Christmas, and how he was doing. "I understand," she had said. "How easy it would be to take it personally, but I would suggest you consider it from another point of view. You gave them your loyalty, commitment, and expertise, in exchange for a paycheck. And as soon as they stop paying you . . . they are not your concern anymore. I know it is hard to see it that way when you are at this stage, but screw it all, Norm. It's their loss."

She may have said all that just to make him feel better about himself, but it worked. Or at least it did when he forced himself to dwell on it. Now that it was over and done, he could. And now that it was over and done, it was a relief. Before, while he had been waiting and counting down the days, he had allowed himself the fantasy that they would get together some morning and realize it was a huge mistake and reinstate them all. But that was never going to happen. It just wasn't how things were done in the real world.

"You guys doing okay?" He asked over his shoulder. Dwayne and Brad were in the back seat and had fallen silent.

"Yeah," they answered together. "But when are we going to get to Santa's village?"

"We're almost there?" he answered. "It's a long way to the North Pole."

C.C. had said other stuff to him too. She had told him that he shouldn't allow all that was happening to affect his self-worth. He had laughed at that. "A man is what he does," he had replied, repeating something his father had always said.

"While I am willing to ignore your chauvinistic, gender-based terminology, I have to disagree with that," C.C. had said with that laugh she used to tease him. "The Norm I know is so much more."

"Like?"

"Like a great father and let's face it; who else could put up with being married to my sister?"

"I bet you say that to all your brothers-in-law."

"You got me there, Norm, but I am serious. Besides, you will get a new job and all of this will just be another page of your life. So, in the meantime, let's make this the best Christmas ever. Are you in?"

"All in," he had agreed and hung up.

"Daddy," Brad interrupted from the back seat.

"Yup?"

"Do you know what I am going to ask Santa for?"

"A new brother?"

"No. I am going to ask Santa to get you a new job."

"Daddy doesn't need Santa to get him a new job," Dwayne joined in. "Daddy could get any job he wanted. Isn't that right, Daddy?"

Norm was more than a little choked up, but he had to laugh. "Sure it is, but if the Big Guy wants to help . . ."

"Well," Dwayne said in his air of self-importance. "I am going to ask Santa for new skates. And a new hockey stick."

"I'm going to ask him for that, too," Brad joined in. "And a Maple Leafs jersey."

Norm said nothing, but did lean over and wink at himself in the rearview mirror. He had it covered.

"Look over there," he said as they turned off the road and headed up the bumpy, snowy driveway to the cottage. "There's Santa's village."

Before them, the cottage sparkled with green and red lights, the old-fashioned kind that were so much warmer. They were strung all along the verandas and around each gable, and around the boles of the trees all the way down to the dock.

"Wow," Dwayne and Brad agreed as they unbuckled their seatbelts and pressed up against the car window. "Wow."

"Look, there's the reindeers in among the trees. Wow."

"And there's Santa, on top of the boat house."

"And there's Frosty."

"Where?"

"Down by the dock."

"Wow."

"Can we go see?"

As soon as the car stopped, they were gone. Norm sat watching them and it just felt right. He might have stayed there longer but the others had filed out and where standing around on the veranda. They were all wearing elf hats and Norm had to smile, even as a tear trickled down his cheek. He got out of the car just as the lights began to blink and twinkle and had to smile. This was his family and all the Jacks in the world could never take that from him.

"When you are done having your girly moment," C.C. walked towards him and handed him a beer. "Get your ass inside. We are about to decorate the tree."

*

The tree had looked so much smaller outside. C.C. and Carol had said it was too big, but Johnnie wouldn't listen. He and Susie had decided on this one and that was that. "I can trim it a little," he had said as he struggled to force it through the door. "Or a lot," he added when he tried to stand it up. It was at least two feet too tall. And it spread out across half the room.

"Or you could knock down a few walls and raise the ceiling." C.C. suggested as she handed him a beer. "Besides, Norm's here now. I am sure that between the two of you, you can figure something out."

"Yes," Mary agreed. "Perhaps we should leave the men to do what they have to do and the rest of us can go into the kitchen. We have so much to get ready."

"And miss all the fun?" Carol nudged Johnnie with her elbow. "I want to sit here and watch these great man-minds at work."

"I have an idea," Norm offered after taking a swig from his beer. "Why don't we take it back outside, throw it away and pick another one."

"Or we could get a nice, fake tree," Buddy suggested as she sipped from her eggnog. Mary had made it and it was perfect, even after C.C. had added a little too much rum.

"No," Gloria said as she came in, shuffling slowly and holding on to Susie. "Let us show some faith in our men. I am sure they will make this the best tree we have ever had, but I agree with Mary. We should go to the kitchen and let them work in peace."

"And reinforce gender stereotypes?" C.C. asked with her tongue in cheek.

"I am not sure what that is supposed to mean," Buddy had to add, "but I, for one, would prefer if our Christmas dinner was edible."

"Children." Mary tried to sound authoritative, but she couldn't keep a straight face. "Let's try to observe a Christmas truce. After all, Santa is coming and I wouldn't want to have to tell him that certain people have been naughty."

"She started it."

"You know," Norm suggested, after they had gone. "We could prop it up at an angle."

"If you are not going to be more helpful, maybe you should join the women."

"C'mon, Johnnie. I am just trying to help."

"If you want to help then grab an end. We will take it outside and trim it."

Getting it back out the door was an effort, but they managed. They dragged it out to the veranda and Norm held it while Johnnie went to get his saw, and his shears. He was determined to make it fit.

"Good job on the lights," Norm offered when he came back. "How did you get them all working?"

"The lights are new. We just took the old bulbs, hollowed them out and stuck them over the new ones."

"Smart."

"It was Joey's idea. He's been working on them since he got here this morning. He even strung most of them, himself."

"A chip off the old block, eh?"

"More of a new and improved version. I didn't think the kid had it in him."

"It's good to hear you say that. So, are you guys going to be okay?"

"Yup, only don't go blabbing it. I want it to be a surprise."

In the kitchen Mary, Buddy, and Carol, all worked in perfect time to the Nutcracker Suite. Turning and bending, and lifting, chopping and dicing, and stirring bowls, while C.C. sat back and winked at Gloria. She had been given her place of honor by the stove where she could oversee everything and offer her comments and observations on all that was happening. Susie sat beside her and readjusted her shawl every time it slipped from her narrow shoulders. The old woman had tears in her eyes, but everyone pretended not to notice.

"I need another pot," Buddy said to no one in particular. "I need to soak the sprouts. C.C., would you mind?"

"And bring out the large bowl," Mary called out as C.C. made her way to the scullery.

"And check on Johnnie," Carol added. "It sounds like he is sawing down the whole forest."

"I do like oysters," Gloria mentioned. "Make sure you put them in the stuffing."

"I already have," Mary answered as she wiped her brow. "In that one." She pointed to the middle dish of three. "It is just the way you like it."

"Good," Gloria nodded. "And is there any bacon in it?"

"There is," Buddy confirmed and held the dish so Gloria could inspect it. "It is exactly how you make it. See."

"Here," Carol held up a spoon as C.C. made her way back. "Taste this and tell me if it needs more sugar."

"What is it supposed to be?"

"Stewed cranberry, but I think it's still too bitter."

"I prefer it that way." C.C. took a taste and grimaced.

"You would," Buddy had to add. "But Norm and I prefer the canned. It's less work."

"You would."

"And what's that supposed to mean."

"Now girls," Mary laughed and stepped between them. "Remember our Christmas truce."

"She started it."

"Did not."

"You know," Mary laughed again. "I have missed this."

"What?" Buddy asked as she opened the oven door to check on the birds.

"All of us being together. I wasn't sure we would be able to do it again, after . . . well, you know."

"After what? When we all found out you weren't the saint you always pretended to be?"

"Well, C.C. I would not have put it so bluntly, but yes."

"There is another way of looking at it," Carol interjected as off-handedly as she could. "If things had been different, we wouldn't have C.C.."

"You have the rare gift," C.C. smiled and stood face to face with her sister-in-law. "Of saying things that can be interpreted so many different ways."

"Thank you, C.C., and I mean them all from the bottom of my heart."

*

"And that," Johnnie decided as he walked around the tree once more, snipping with his shears like a barber. "Is perfect."

"Now we just got to get the damn thing in and decorate it."

"Not us, Bro. Joey and the little guys are going to do that."

"Okay, then. That's leaves only one more thing."

"And that is?"

"To crack open a few more brewskis."

"I'm down with that."

After they dragged the tree inside, they went back outside and sat on the veranda smiling at each other.

"Happy Christmas, Norm."

"Happy Christmas, Johnnie. You doing okay?"

"Great. Why do you ask?"

"Oh, you know. Being up here again after . . . you know."

"Yeah, I have been thinking about that."

"And?"

"I don't blame him anymore. He had every right to ask me what he did."

"And you had every right to say no."

"I know that now."

They clinked their bottles together and stood looking in the window. Joey, Dwayne and Brad were busy. They had unentangled all the lights and were stringing them around the tree. Gloria and Susie had joined them. Gloria was sitting in her rocking chair with a box on her lap. She reached in and pulled out another old ornament and handed it to Brad. Then she reached for another and smiled at the memories it evoked.

It began to snow, softly and gently, but Johnnie and Norm stayed where they were. Standing vigil in the night, watching their families.

"And this is what it is all about," Norm laughed and shook his head. "We just have to remember this when life turns on us again."

"Don't get all emotional on me."

"I'm not. It's just we have all been through the ringer, lately. I'm just trying to put it all in perspective."

"Good luck with that, but if you want my opinion; I'd wait until it's all said and done. With this family, there's bound to be a few more twists and turns before it is over."

"Are you two going to join us?" Carol asked and held the door open for them. "We need someone tall to hang the mistletoe."

Chapter 23

Christmas morning was as beautiful as any one of them could have hoped for. The sun was low in the sky, but it was bright and cheering. There had been a light fall of fresh snow and against the deep blue sky, everything around the cottage looked renewed. Because it had been too cold to use the bedrooms in the boathouse, sleeping arrangements had to be improvised. Johnnie and Carol, Buddy and Norm, all had their usual rooms while Mary and Gloria shared. As did C.C. and Susie who was not just a bed hog, but a night thrasher, too. Joey and the two younger boys made beds on the floor of the living room and during the night, Brad had rolled in among the presents under the tree.

They woke in dribs and drabs and made their way to the kitchen where Carol had been busy making coffee, orange juice, and French toast that they could cover with the maple syrup that one of Gloria's neighbors had dropped off.

"You didn't have to go to all this trouble," Mary told Carol when she came down and began to fuss with all the pots and pans that were primed and ready. Everything was in order and everything smelled wonderful.

"It was no trouble at all," Carol lied and smirked. It had been difficult trying to function in the little space that was not in use. "Besides, the alternative would have been murder."

"Excuse me?"

"Your son was snoring all night. It was a case of get up and make breakfast, or put a pillow over his face."

"Well, I think you made the right decision."

"Of course she did," Buddy agreed as she came in and checked the oven and rearranged the pots on the stove. "Carol always makes the right decisions."

"If that were true, I'd be in Algarve right now."

"Isn't that somewhere in Portugal?" Mary asked, not understanding the joke. "Why on earth would you want to spend Christmas there?"

"I don't know," Norm piped in. He was standing in the doorway scratching his stomach. "Sitting on the beach, drinking wine—it could be alright."

"I wouldn't care for it," Mary said with a touch of disdain.

"It was a joke," Carol explained.

"Just not a very funny one," Buddy added.

Before Carol could react to that, C.C. brushed past Norm and headed straight for the coffee, almost elbowing Carol out of her way as she passed.

"My, you are looking very disheveled this morning. Did you not have a good night?"

"Your daughter should be made to sleep in a straight jacket."

"Why? What the hell were you two up to?" Carol asked, tongue in cheek.

"Carol!" Buddy and Mary chimed in, sharing their mock shock.

"Yeah, Carol." C.C. joined in as she stood beside them, with one hand on her hip. She raised her coffee mug with the other to hide her smile. "In this family we make it a point to differentiate between being gay and being a pedophile."

"C.C.," Mary and Buddy admonished, almost in unison. "Don't even say such a thing."

"Why are you guys talking about pedophilia?" Johnnie asked as he came in and looked around at them all. "Can we not just have a good, old fashioned family Christmas for once?"

"That would be nice," Gloria agreed as she wandered in and began looking for something.

"Can I help?" Buddy offered.

"Help with what?"

"What you are looking for."

"And what is that?"

"Right," Carol announced after they had all exchanged knowing glances. "You two," she pointed at Johnnie and Norm, "will serve the kids and the rest of us will sit down and tuck in."

"Why can't they come and get their own?"

"Because it is Christmas."

"It's too early," Susie yawned as she walked in and went straight over and wrapped her arms around Gloria.

*

At C.C.'s suggestion, she, Johnnie and Carol, Buddy and Norm, would all accompany Mary. She wanted to go out to the island and lay the fresh flowers she had asked C.C. to pick out. C.C. had decided on carnations, lilies, gladiolas and tulips, all neatly wrapped in ruffles of white paper, held together with golden ribbon. The younger kids had been instructed to stay with Gloria and, if they behaved, they could open their gifts when the others got back. Joey had gone back to sleep, but Susie was a little miffed at not being invited.

"I would prefer if you stayed here," Mary had told her. "As I have something to discuss with the adults."

Carol had been about to get involved, but C.C. got there first. "It's okay, Susie," she soothed. "I'm sure that Grandma has her reasons."

"And my reason," Mary explained after they had stood in silence for a while, looking down at the new flowers in the snow. "Is I wanted to tell you about a gift your father left for you all." She paused as she looked at each one in turn. "I was contacted by one of the attorneys who is looking after his estate and your father has left a considerable amount of money to be shared among you. I was only told about this yesterday because your father wanted it to be a Christmas gift." She smiled, but she had tears in her eyes as she looked down at the flowers. "He has left over five million dollars, but there is a stipulation; the money can only be used in what the lawyer described as 'joint ventures.' And your father left instructions that I was to oversee it all." She paused and looked at each one of them again. They were shocked, but in a good way.

"Now, as you all know, I have no experience in things like this so I will need each one of you to come together and help me do what is best. It was your father's stated wish that the money be used to bring you together rather than drive you apart and I would like to think we will be able to honor that."

None of them spoke. They were all wandering through their own thoughts, but Johnnie reached out and squeezed Carol's hand. Buddy looked up at Norm and smiled, while C.C. stood back and watched them all with a knowing smile.

"It has been a very difficult time for all of us," Mary continued. "And I know we have all struggled in our own ways to come to terms with it. Hopefully, this can be what brings us all back together. And let's begin by sharing another moment remembering a man who never stopped loving each and every one of us."

She fell silent as they gathered around her. They all looked down at the flowers in the snow. They looked so bright and hopeful in the great white absolution they were all feeling.

*

After they had eaten far too much, and relayed the leftovers back to the kitchen where Carol organized them into a put-away crew, and a wash-up crew, Joey was appointed Santa's helper. He put on the elf hat that had been a part of family Christmases since his father was a child. Jake had given it to Johnnie the first Christmas after Buddy was born, when they began to give out the gifts together.

Joey gave Dwayne and Brad their gifts first—as they had waited so patiently—and they were not disappointed. New hockey equipment from their father, a few video games, and socks, gloves and underwear from their mother. They wanted to go out and play shinny on the lake, but were coaxed into waiting until everybody else had opened their gifts.

"To C.C., from Santa," Joey read, after the boys had settled down, and handed his aunt a small package wrapped in the business section of The Globe and Mail.

C.C. pretended to become engrossed with an article until everybody groaned. "Open it, already."

"What could it be?" she asked as she tore it open. Inside was a corporate Barbie doll dressed in a grey suit, complete with a business bag and a flip phone. And it was mint-in-box.

"Ho, ho, ho," she laughed and held it up while she posed for the obligatory pictures. "And thank you, Carol."

"Hey, it's a secret Santa. Why do you think I had anything to do with it?"

"Because nobody else reads that newspaper."

"À la Norm, du Père Noël." Joey managed in his best school French and handed his uncle his gift, in a plain brown wrapper. He opened it and gestured like he was going to throw it into the wood stove.

"Let us see," everyone clamored while Johnnie sat back and smirked.

"Fine," Norm agreed and posed with his Montreal hockey shirt. "As if it wasn't bad enough that I am about to become an unemployed bum, but now this?"

"To Buddy, from Santa," Joey continued when they all stopped laughing and handed his aunt a bag from the store Jerome worked at. Inside were a pair of lime green yoga pants, a box of chamomile tea, a worry-beads bracelet, and a gift voucher from the store.

Buddy wrinkled her brow and placed each item on the floor in front of her. "Thank you, Santa, for the mixed messages."

There was an awkward silence so Joey quickly moved on and handed his father an old shoe box with the Hudson's Bay company logo on the top. "To Johnnie, from Santa."

"Wow," Johnnie laughed. "The box is nearly as old as I am."

"Just open it," Gloria spoke up for the first time. She had been sitting in her rocking chair, smiling and nodding when anyone looked over at her.

"Aww," everybody laughed as Johnnie took out a pair of old-fashioned slippers, and a pipe.

"Was this your idea of a joke?" he asked C.C.

"Nothing to do with me, Bro, though I wish I had thought of it."

Carol got a tee-shirt with Tony Danza on it, asking: "Who's the Boss?" She'd had a crush on him when she was younger. She put it on and posed with her other gift, a coffee mug with the same question.

Gloria got a framed picture of them all in caricature, decorated with dried pasta in different colors. A few pieces had fallen off in the packing, but Gloria hardly noticed that.

"And this one," Joey read from the back of an envelope. "Is for Mary and Gloria, from Santa and all the elves."

"Would you like me to open it?" Mary asked Gloria, but she didn't answer. She was still far too engrossed and was touching each face in her picture.

"Very well, then." Mary opened the envelope and read the hand-written voucher. She began to laugh and cry at the same time as she made her way over to Gloria.

"What is it?"

"Read what it says."

"I don't have my glasses."

"They are on your head, but never mind. I will read it. 'This entitles the bearers to a Caribbean tour.' Oh, Gloria. We are going on a cruise."

"And," Joey continued as he reached behind the tree and pulled out a large, rectangular, flat box. "To Susie, from Santa."

It was the painting Gloria had promised to give her at the end of the summer, and it had been professionally framed.

"And finally," Joey read after everyone settled down again. He had reached under the tree and pulled out a large green garbage bag with a cardboard cutout of a Christmas bow taped around the neck.

"To Joey, from Santa."

"Open it," Carol insisted as Johnnie stood back again and smirked.

"What the . . ." Joey asked as he pulled out his father's old tool belt, a well-worn pair of working gloves, and an inflatable toy hammer.

"And, if you can figure out which end to use," Johnnie laughed as he took the little hammer and turned it over in his large hands, "you just might be allowed to use a real one."

After they had played hockey on the ice for almost two hours, everyone was exhausted. It had been Dwayne, Brad, Joey, and Susie against the adults. The kids had won easily and the adults had been quick to agree that it was all Norm's fault. In his defense, Norm pointed out that it was down to him having to wear the Montreal shirt. Everyone played along with that and no one mentioned that while Buddy had played in goal, she hadn't managed to stop a single shot from her kids, including a dribbler from Brad that she had accidently managed to kick over the line.

When they got back, Buddy, C.C., and Mary had organized a buffet supper and while everyone said they weren't hungry, it was picked clean in minutes. After that, there was little to do but relax and enjoy the evening together. Johnnie and Joey had brought in enough firewood to keep them going until spring and no one had any reason to be anywhere else.

"This is perfect," Mary announced as she looked around at them all. "We have to be the luckiest women in the world to have you all here with us again. Isn't that right, Gloria?"

"Aww," everyone groaned, except Joey and the younger boys. They were busy with a video game.

"We are," Mary added when Gloria didn't respond, "but I still can't wait to get away on our cruise. I just hope Santa didn't go broke getting it for us."

"He had lots of help," Buddy winked at the others. "And he knew somebody that knew somebody," she added while smiling in C.C.'s direction. "I think the Easter Bunny and the Tooth Fairy might have chipped in."

"Well, there's no guessing who helped him with my present," Norm nudged Johnnie.

"Nothing to do with me, Bro. Santa just asked if you had been naughty or nice."

"I guess he asked you the same about me?" C.C. asked Carol.

"It wasn't me. I wish it was, but it wasn't."

"Who else could it have been. It had all the hallmarks of humor and intelligence. Nobody else here has any of those things."

"Excuse me," Buddy interjected.

"Was it you?"

"No, it was Norm, although I did help him find it."

"Really?"

"Yup."

"This is fun," Susie joined in. "Let's see if we can guess who got Dad the slippers."

"Right, as if you didn't know."

"I do know, but it wasn't me."

They spent the rest of the evening joking, laughing, and playing games. The fire crackled and danced, and the lights on the tree jigged on and off in concertina time. Gloria had fallen asleep in her chair and Mary sat beside her, gently stroking the back of the older woman's hand.

Johnnie and Norm stood by the window, sipping on a few beers and talking about the future while Carol squatted on the floor with Buddy and Susie, playing cards and laughing every chance they got. C.C. sat back and watched them all. It was almost perfect. Almost, but not quite.

She decided to take a walk and slipped away unnoticed. She bundled up and made her way back to where the flowers lay. She just needed a little time on her own. She had done everything that had been asked of her and now she just needed a little time to think about her own future.

She was feeling alone but unafraid in the great silence of the night when her phone buzzed in her pocket. Heather had texted her. *I just made a Christmas wish*, it read. *Would you like to know what it was?*

Sure, C.C. typed back

I wished that this would be the last Christmas we did not spend together.

Chapter 24

"That went well," Carol ventured as they drove away from the cottage. Joey and Susie had decided to ride with C.C., giving her and Johnnie some time alone. They had hardly had time to talk about all that had happened.

"You think so?"

"Yeah, don't you?"

"Yeah, I think it did."

"But?"

"There's no buts, I am just still absorbing it all."

"Good stuff?"

"Yeah, babe. It's all good."

"Good, because when we get back to the city, it's straight to work for me. I have a proposal ready for Ben, and now that we have a way to finance it. Well . . ."

"Ben? You guys are on a first name basis already?"

"Would you prefer if I called him Sugar Daddy?"

"I remember when you used to call me that."

"Things change, Johnnie. Get used to it. Besides, now that you will be sleeping with your boss, I think I am going to start calling you Sugar Boy."

"I could be okay with all of that, except it kind of makes me feel like what I do is about to become more of a hobby than a real job."

"You don't get it, do you? The real reason women strive to be successful is so they can have boy-toys.

Luckily for you, I happen to like the construction type—it's a hangover from my Village People days."

"I can be cool with that."

"Good." Carol reached over and put her hand on his arm. He looked like he had come to terms with everything that had happened and he finally looked at peace with himself. For now, she smiled to herself. Happily ever after was something that only happened in books, but she was okay with happy for now. "Though I might have to get you a cop uniform, and maybe even an Indian headdress."

"Whatever you say, boss," he pretended to groan and reached over and pulled her towards him.

"By the way." She added after she had readjusted her seatbelt. "Nice moves with Joey's gift."

"Hey, that had nothing to do with me. That was all Santa's doing."

"I know," Carol smiled to herself and rested her head against his shoulder. "So? Are we good?"

"For now. At least until the next curveball life decides to throw at us."

"And the whole business with your father?"

"Yeah, that. I guess I just made far too big a deal about that . . . you know, because it was that last thing we got to talk about. It wasn't something he should have asked me to do, and I should have been able to let it go at that."

"Yeah, on both counts." She agreed, but was tempted to try to get him to say more. He would, when he was ready and she knew him well enough to let him get there on his own.

"Did I ever tell you what C.C. said when we threw Jake's ashes over the lake?" he asked when they were settled again.

"No, but I can imagine."

"She said: 'Let the wind take all that should be forgotten and leave us only with what should be remembered.'"

"C.C. said that? Wow, there might be more to that girl than I ever gave her credit for."

"Not really. Some of the ashes blew back into our faces."

"Now that sounds more like the C.C. we have all come to love."

*

"So? Are you happy with your new job?" Buddy asked Norm once they got back on the main road. The kids had plugged in and were not paying any attention.

"What do you think?"

"I think you should be, if it is what you really want to do. I just hope that you are not doing it because you are feeling pressured. You know, by my family, and all."

"Thanks, but I'm pretty sure about this and I think Johnnie and I can work well together. We will be a good partnership and I think I can bring a lot to the show. I won't be able to draw out the same money but with the severance package, that won't be an issue for a while."

Buddy thought about correcting him. She was the partner and he was now her employee, but she decided to let it go. "Well, as long as you are happy."

"I am, but what about you?"

"I'll be fine."

"Will you?"

"I will, though I have to admit that I am a bit envious of everybody getting to start new lives while I keep on trucking with the kids. But I guess that's my lot—at least for a few more years."

"Anything I can do to help?"

"There is. You can keep on being the man I don't deserve."

"Aww, shucks."

∗

"What are you thinking about?" Susie asked after they had driven in silence for a while. She had 'called' shotgun and Joey had to settle for the back seat. He didn't mind and had gone back to sleep with his toy hammer clutched to his chest. He even had a smile on his face.

"What am I thinking about, now that's a very good question. I was thinking about my own life, if you must know."

"You must be so happy about Heather?"

"I am, but there is more to it than that. I have been rethinking my life lately and I have been trying to figure out what it is that would really make me happy."

"Doesn't Heather make you happy?"

"Oh, she does, but I am talking about more than that."

"Like what?"

"Like when I was younger and tried to find happiness in other people, but I never could. I really thought that would change after I came out. It didn't. If anything, it got worse. Then I met Heather and she made me realize something: I had become far too dependent on what other people thought of me. And I spent far too much time and energy pretending otherwise. I have given that a lot of thought for the last few months and I am finally coming to a decision."

"And what is that?"

"I think I should just like myself for who I already am. I am a damn good person, a great V.P., the world's best sister, and daughter. Even if I have to say so myself."

"I always thought that, and you are the world's best aunt."

"Damn right Susie. You are so damn right, all the time."

"C.C." Susie asked when they finished laughing at themselves. "Is Gloria going to be okay?"

*

The morning after everyone had left, Mary quietly made her way down to the kitchen. She would make tea and toast and bring it up to Gloria who would be tired. Having everybody visit was great, but Gloria was a stubborn old woman and had over done it; fussing around with the kids, getting involved in every game they had wanted to play. That was all well and good, but now she would be exhausted and Mary would have to look after her.

She didn't mind. She had enjoyed every minute of it all; having the family around and feeling herself restored in their eyes. However, there was still Gloria to think about. What was to become of her? How would she be able to deal with it all? From now on, life would be very different for all of them.

When she entered the kitchen all the lights were on. The table had been set for two and the old china tea pot sat in the middle—the one that Gloria only used for special occasions.

"So, sleepy head? You finally decided to get up?" Gloria was standing by the stove. She had scrambled eggs and fried some bacon. She was looking very pleased with herself—in fact she looked totally reinvigorated.

"Gloria?" Mary managed, but was too surprised to say anything else.

"Yes, my dear? What is the matter? You look like you have seen a ghost."

"Well I suppose I have. I seem to be looking at the ghost of what you used to be."

"Oh, dear. Have I become so transparent?"

"No, I didn't mean it that way. I just mean . . . well, I haven't seen you like this since . . ."

"Since Jake died?"

"Well . . . yes."

"Yes, I suppose you are right, but never mind all of that now. Breakfast is ready and we wouldn't want our eggs to get cold. Would we?"

Mary nodded because she couldn't think of anything else to do. She thought about offering to help, but Gloria had already carried their plates to the table and had gone back for the toast. "Sit," she reminded Mary when she came back. "Sit down and eat."

Mary sat as Gloria poured their tea with a smile and a flourish. She then sat and began to eat with vigor and relish. She had made them two eggs a piece and four pieces of bacon. She had eaten half of it while Mary was still nibbling at the corners of hers.

"What's the matter, have you gone off my cooking?"

"Of course not. It's just that I am a bit surprised."

"At what?"

"Well, lately you have seemed so . . . lethargic. I was beginning to think the worst."

"That I was on death's door step?"

"Don't make light of such things, but yes. The way you have been the last few weeks . . . well, you can understand why I was getting so concerned."

"Oh that. Yes, I am sorry for having to put you through all of that, but it was the only way I could think of."

Mary was at a total loss for words and Gloria reached across and put her hand on her daughter-in-law's arm. "Forgive me, Mary but it was the only way I could see it working."

"Only way you could see what working?"

"Mary, you have now become the head of this family. This Christmas proved that. I just had to make it seem like I was no longer capable."

"So, this was all a ploy?"

"Yes."

"And you felt you had to keep it all from me?"

"Yes. I felt it would be better if you believed it too. That way you would be far more convincing."

"And you don't think I could have been trusted with your scheme?"

"Oh, Mary. Let's not replough old fields. I decided that it would be better if you took on the whole job believing that you had to."

"I am not sure how I feel about that."

"Well, I think you should feel happy about it. And I think you could feel relieved that I am not going to die—at least not too soon."

"So, it is a case of 'the queen is dead long live the queen'?"

"I think it would be more like The Dread Pirate Roberts – you know, when the old pirate pretended to be dead while helping the new one settle into the job. Now please eat your breakfast so that we can get on with the rest of the day."

Mary did.

*

Gloria knew that Mary would need some time to absorb what she had just told her. A part of her would be offended but after she had enough time to digest it all, she would come to see that Gloria was right.

She was. Her life had been a hard teacher, but she had learned her lessons well. And she had succeeded in rectifying some of the damage done by her old mistakes.

It had been so wrong of her not to tell Jake when his father was dying. She hadn't because Harry had not wanted that; he and Jake had become so estranged and Harry had just wanted to die in peace. At the time, Gloria only wanted to respect his wishes and did not give enough thought to the impact it would have on Jake. He had not been able to say goodbye to his father. That was when he became so embittered and she had been forced to watch as his anger and resentments had distorted him. And she had to watch again as the ramifications of that had spilled down through the generations that followed.

To his credit, Jake had come to terms with all of that before he died and only wanted to try to make things right with Mary and his children. It was one of the first things they had talked about after he had been diagnosed. He would come and make whatever peace he could with them, but after that?

Together, he and Gloria had hatched the whole plan. He wanted to leave money, but he had wanted Gloria to oversee it. They had disagreed on that until she had been able to convince him how much Mary would benefit from being the one to do it. It would give her a chance to redeem herself, and after the truth about C.C. had been revealed, she really needed that. Neither of them had seen that one coming, but Mary had blotted her page in so many other ways.

All in all, it had worked out rather well for everybody involved.

"Who else knew?" Mary asked after she had sat in silence for a while.

"Just C.C. and Susie, but they both agreed to play along."

Susie had played her part without question. She was still at that age where she could trust and, with her innocence, she was perfect at gathering information. There were times when Gloria had to ask herself if she was manipulating the child, but she had always arrived at the same conclusion: the end justified the means.

C.C. was a different story. She was looking to redefine herself and, after finding out about her father, needed something to help her feel that she could be a central part of the family again.

C.C. had been reluctant when Gloria had first broached the issue, but Gloria knew how to deal with that. All she had to do was to make it seem like the right cause; one that could only be achieved by someone with C.C.'s skills and talents.

She had thought about involving Johnnie, but he was busy dealing with his own issues and was best left alone. Johnnie would find his way through—he always did. He was the eldest and his sense of duty would always compel him.

Buddy? Buddy had enough to do and would always struggle with what really was and wasn't. It was just the way things were for a middle child.

Family dynamics, Gloria had often smiled to herself but there were times when she had doubted herself and what she was doing. But, as she often reminded herself, family was not a democracy and someone had to take charge. Even someone as flawed as she.

"I see. And what will happen when the others find out?"

"What can they say? What can anybody say?"

Mary finished her breakfast while Gloria drank her tea and looked through the cards her great grandchildren had made for her. Each one brought a different smile to her face. Each one was like a warm embrace. Susie's was her favorite, but she would never let on.

When Mary finally finished eating, Gloria rose and began to clear the table. When she was done, she stood by her kitchen window and looked out at the frozen lake. The flowers had been dusted with drifting snow but could still be seen—a bright splash of colors in the white landscape.

She'd had a different dream last night. This time, after she had broken through the ice and had reached down, she had been able to take hold of Jake's hand. Effortlessly, she had been able to raise him to the surface. He had emerged from the ice like he was being reborn and stood for a moment and smiled at her. He was neither cold nor wet. In fact, he seemed to glow.

Without saying anything he reached forward and touched her cheek. His fingers were warm and soft. He then took her in his arms and held her for a moment that made everything inside of her feel light. He slowly let go and smiled. He then turned towards the moon that was already heading for the trees on the far side of the lake. He turned back once more to smile. Then he slowly floated up and away. She wanted to reach out to him, but she knew it wasn't time. She knew he had to go and she would follow later.

Acknowledgments

As well as the usual suspects, Lou Aronica and all the good people at The Story Plant, I would like to acknowledge the most important contributors to any writer's work—the readers. Without them, none of this would have resonance.

About the Author

Peter Murphy was born in Killarney where he spent his first three years before his family had to move to Dublin. Growing up in the verdant braes of Templeogue, Peter was schooled by the De La Salle brothers in Churchtown where he played rugby for "The Wine and Gold." He also played football (soccer) in secret! After that, he graduated and studied the Humanities in Grogan's under the guidance of Scot's corner and the bar staff, Paddy, Tommy and Sean. Murphy financed his education by working summers on the buildings sites of London. He also tramped the roads of Europe playing music and living without a care in the world.

But his move to Canada changed all of that. He only came over for a while and ended up living there for more than thirty years. He took a day job and played music in the bars at night until the demands of family life intervened. Having raised his children and packed them off to university, Murphy answered the long-ignored internal voice and began to write. He has published five novels so far and has begun work on a new one. Nowadays, he lives in beautiful Lisbon with his wife Eduarda and their well-read dog, Baxter.